FINDING
JOY

A simple thank you can never be enough to express my gratitude to my extraordinary Mum, Brothers and Sister.

Or to my incredible friends Duncan, Katherine, Gordon, Michael and Matthew. To Anne and Ken for their unwavering support. To Lucy, Sheena and to the private medical team who have been imperative to my recovery.

Finally, to Skye… my very own Dog.

Website – www.morven-may.co.uk
Twitter – @MorvenMay
Facebook – @morvenmay

FINDING
JOY

MORVEN-MAY
MACCALLUM

BROWN
DOG
BOOKS

Published under licence by Brown Dog Books and The Self-Publishing Partnership, 7 Green Park Station, Bath BA1 1JB

www.selfpublishingpartnership.co.uk

ISBN printed book: 978-1-78545-157-7
ISBN e-book: 978-1-78545-158-4

Cover design by Kevin Rylands
Internal design by Andrew Easton

Printed and bound by CPI Group (UK) Ltd, Croydon CR0 4YY

Chapter One

'Is that right, Joyce? Have you been feeling a bit down lately?'

'I'm fine,' I tell him, resisting the urge to glare at my aunt for bringing up the subject.

'Can you tell me the name of a programme you like?' the doctor asks, watching me closely.

I stare at him blankly, not least because I cannot see the point of his question, but also because I literally cannot think of a single programme. I'm painfully aware of the seconds ticking by from the doctor's oversized and overly loud clock on the wall and the pressure of both the doctor's and my aunt's gaze is not helping.

I finally manage to give him the name of a programme which I can't remember watching recently and I do so with a shrug from one of my shoulders.

'Good,' he says, running his hand across his greying and neatly trimmed beard. 'Tell me, when you look around you or when you're outside, how do things seem?'

'What do you mean?' I ask hesitantly.

'Do you see your surroundings in black and grey? Like all the colour's gone and dimmed?'

I'm pretty certain he's trying to be helpful, kind even, but I'm wondering if this is a trick question or whether he just wasn't listening before when I told him that my eyes are overly sensitive to light. To me, nothing is dim. Even on the most overcast day in which the middle of the day is as dark as dusk, I still find it too bright. The colours aren't dim – they're blinding.

'No,' I say, resisting the urge to cross my arms.

'That's good,' he says, looking reassured by my answer. 'Often people who are depressed say that they feel as though all the colour has been drained from the world and you were able to tell me about a programme you like. You were quite defensive about it which shows you have an interest in it, so that's very good. I'm going to put a note in your records because I think it might be worth your usual doctor to investigate the possibility of ME or CFS, whichever term you prefer.'

I should have pointed out that his question was flawed. What he should have asked was whether the colours were lifeless. That would have got an entirely different answer altogether and a one-sided shoulder shrug is not defensive – it's practically the definition of uncertainty or indifference. I know this because two years ago I was all but packed and ready to go to university to study psychology, and one of the many books I read in preparation for my degree was on body language: clearly the doctor and I didn't buy the same textbook. But both the doctor and my aunt looked pleased so I never said anything. Besides, my brain doesn't work like that anymore; it only comes up with these revelations a good twenty minutes to a day after they're needed, when I'm a good ten miles from the hospital, sitting in a garden centre coffee shop where there is no feasible way of telling him his mistake.

It's become a ritual for my aunt and me to come here after my doctor's appointments. It's pretty much the only time I leave the house. I'm sitting at a corner table, where I can watch all the goings-on around me. I like it here because no one can sit behind me. It makes me nervous when they can: I can't see what's happening. My aunt's left me here on my own while she goes to get our refreshments. It's the lesser of two negatives because standing for any length of time drains me of energy and leaves me liable to the odd fainting, but I don't like being left on my own. It's the hidden secret of being ill. People don't realise or think of what it must be like to be trapped inside your own home for months on end without seeing anyone beyond your immediate family and the postie. Just think how quiet it is when no one's around and it's just you on your own at home. Nothing moves unless you make it. Imagine that still quietness enduring for months, years. And then you're thrust into the throng of the world you've been excluded from, banished like a disgraced child of ill fate. The large coffee shop is, by anyone's standards (excluding my own), quiet, but to me the noise of the people here is deafening. The whoosh of the machines and the clatter of cutlery are sharp against my sensitive hearing. There's movement everywhere, all around me, pushing in on me. It's like being caught in a storm of hailstones: there's no escaping its sharp assault.

Through the ruckus I hear a booming laugh. My eyes scan the tables for the owner because I'm sure I know that laughter. It's not one that's easily forgotten. I can feel myself sinking deeper into my seat, as though squishing my insides might hide me from the person I've spotted…. inevitably it fails. His face lights up with a broad smile and he waves enthusiastically. I try to smile back, but it's been so long that my muscles aren't cooperating and I'm not entirely sure how big a smile I've shown, so give a small wave which I immediately regret because he takes it as an invitation to come over and there's nowhere to escape to. I'm trapped against the wall and the table, me and my stupid anxieties.

I'm so irrationally eager not to be seen that I even consider going out of the fire exit which is right behind me, but I'm not sure if it's got an alarm and it would be blatantly obvious what I was doing if it does.

'Joy, how are you?' Logan says brightly. He seems genuinely happy to see me, which makes me feel even worse because in any other circumstances I would be delighted to see him, too.

I know it's stupid. I'm eighteen which means it's been two years. They all know I'm sick but still I try my best to pretend otherwise when I see them. I shower, I put on make-up, I wear clothes. But I was tired yesterday, really tired and sore, so I never showered which makes it a day or two ago since I last did. My aunt said that it was a good thing for the doctor to see that I was too tired to shower. She told me not to wear make-up: 'Don't hide how sick you are: they need to see. Maybe then they will take us seriously.'

'I'm fine, thanks. How are you?' I say, tucking my auburn hair behind my ear and away from my eyes: a perk of it being unwashed is that I know it will stay there.

'Yeah I'm good. How've you been lately?' he asks, his eyes moving to the plaster on the inside of my elbow from where they've taken my blood. (Another reason for the coffee and cake shop; I tend to faint a little while after they've drawn phials of blood from me.)

'Fine. I've been seeing a specialist at the hospital,' I tell him. Logan and I are the same age but somehow he looks different since the last time I saw him about eight months ago. I think his face has slimmed, become more defined perhaps, while mine remains unchanged. He's in the same clothes I've always been used to seeing him in: jeans and a shirt, neither fancy nor casual.

He has brown hair and bright brown eyes that all the girls in school used to comment on.

'They still don't know what's wrong?' Logan asks. I don't like it when people ask this question because I'm never sure if there's a note of scepticism in their voice or whether I'm imagining it.

'No,' I say, clasping my hands tightly together under the table.

'Did you get my message? I'm going to be about for a while if you're free to meet up?' he asks eagerly.

'Sorry, I…haven't checked my phone.'

'Oh well, I sent it a couple of weeks ago so it probably never sent right,' he says dismissively.

'Yeah, I…haven't checked my phone,' I say awkwardly as my aunt appears with a tray with two cups and a plate of sugar-filled cake for us to share.

'I better get back, but if you're free I can come round sometime,' Logan says, smiling brightly.

'Sure,' I say with a horrible swoop of both dread and excitement in my stomach.

***

My aunt left for work twenty minutes ago. She has her own business as an electrician which comes with the benefit of her being able to come to all my doctor's appointments, but it means she's constantly out of the house and often she doesn't come home until late, and with my older cousin and younger sister away at uni and college, I practically live alone…with the silence and stillness and the most lazy dog known to humankind. I can't say I blame the poor thing: I think we both did more than a lifetime of exercise before I became ill, so he's earned the rest.

In the dining room/my new bedroom, I sit on the edge of the sofa bed my aunt bought for me. We have a love-hate relationship, this sofa bed and I, because sleeping in it results from me being too unwell to climb the stairs, but it being here means that I don't have to. Although the room's mine to use, there are still parts of it which show the room's origins: the ornaments and picture above the old fireplace, the sheepskin rug which lies in front of it, and the built-in bookcases on either side are filled with my aunt's books and trinkets.

I finally spot my phone and the charger under a capsized pile of books on the floor. It's been so long since I've needed my phone that I have to charge it for a good ten minutes before it will even turn on. A part of me wonders who else might have messaged me and I pick it up with intrigue when it starts bleeping. I have two messages. Rather disappointingly, one is from the phone company promoting their latest phones, and the other is from Logan. There's nothing new in it; it simply reads: *Hi Joy, I'm heading up the road in the next week or two if you want to meet up?*

I put my phone back on the arm of the couch and look out of the window. There are fields as far as the eye can see, with the mountains I used to walk up at the weekend in the distance. I'm not sure what to do. I'm torn with indecision over whether or not to reply. I shake my head in disapproval of myself. It never used to be like this. I used to be decisive. I knew what I wanted and I always knew what to do and, whatever the consequences were, I was more than capable of overcoming them. Now the simplest of questions become a barrage of possible consequences that I'm no longer able to overcome with ease. 'Do you want a cup of tea?' is easy enough: my mind says yes but then the shadow on my shoulder tells me that if I have a cup of tea at this time of day then I will need the bathroom in middle of the night: which you'll soon learn can be a dangerous thing for me nowadays. I can now understand and sympathise with the procrastinations of the elderly which the young find so tiresome.

I know the outcome of messaging him will be a visit which will mean showering, putting on make-up and clothes, all in the attempt to look and smell more like a human rather than a ripening corpse. I'm not lazy – I swear it, I used to walk up those mountains you know. But seeing people I know means pasting over the cracks which show my infirmity, and pretending I'm not as sick as I am is exhausting. It results in me sleeping down here and I hate sleeping down here. I rub my tired eyes, my brain feeling fuzzy from exhaustion. I sigh as I discard the notion of replying to him later because I know I will forget – my memory has become as impaired as my body. With reluctance I pick up my phone and send a quick message.

I wander along the hall of my aunt's cottage to the kitchen and put on the kettle, preparing my cup as I wait for it to boil. My aunt's cottage is deceptively spacious but it's still a cottage. It used to be hectic with all four of us living here. My cousin used to complain about it being too small, but I'm glad of its neatness now. It means there's less walking required to get from one room to the next. It's only once the waters stopped bubbling that I notice my aunt's filled the kettle to the top; I stare at it for a long time, deliberating. I grab the handle of the kettle with both hands and lift it from its holder. It's so heavy it feels as though I'm holding a sack of sand at arm's reach; my muscles ache as I position the kettle over my cup. I try to pour it, but my arms start shaking so violently that I pour boiling water all over the worktop, panic welling in my stomach as I realise I don't have the strength to tip the kettle back upright. Somehow I manage to put the kettle onto the worktop, but I've spilt half its contents on the floor, down the cupboard doors and down myself, the heat burning my legs before the material turns cool. I look at the mess I've made, my breathing heavy. It never used to be like this; I don't know what I've become.

'Here, let me take that for you,' the lorry driver offers.

'I can carry it,' I say confidently, picking up the large, square hay bale and carrying it up the slope and into the barn.

'You've got a strong lass there. What is she, eight, nine?' the lorry driver says to my grandad.

'She's eight. Just think how strong she'll be when she's older.'

I can't leave this for my aunt to see and I'll forget to do it later, so I pick up the kitchen towel and begin soaking up the water I've spilt with weak and trembling arms. I can barely see what I'm doing for the tears in my eyes. The places where the boiling water spilt down my legs don't hurt anymore, not compared with the pain in my insides. I find another towel and crouch down to dab at the water on the tiled floor, I almost want to laugh at my stupidity. Now I'm down here, I'm not convinced I can get back up.

It took some hard negotiating between the edge of the worktop, table and the muscles in my legs and arms to get back up. On the plus side, I did manage to fill the majority of my cup up. In my dining room/bedroom my phone's flashing to show that there's a new message. Unsurprisingly, it's from Logan: *Wednesday, around three?*

I think I might be pushing my luck in saying yes because it doesn't give me much time to rest beforehand, but the chances are that he'll only be in the area for a week or two anyway, and I would rather get it out the way, so I message him back saying yes.

Chapter Two

The top five things, in no particular order, that the chronically ill give up on first:

- Showering – I know, a lot of you shower-every-day types have just shrivelled up into your shower caps but hear me out. For the non-sick people out there, showering is a pleasant act, but think about it for a moment: think what it is you're asking from your body. You have to stand for anywhere between five and (for you shower-lovers) thirty minutes. To wash your hair, you must extend your arms above your head and rub the shampoo into your hair. Then you have to rinse and start the whole process again only with the conditioner. And don't even get me started on the body wash! And because the heat from the shower (even when I've set it to cold) seems to drain me of energy, showering takes an entire day's allowance of energy which, to me, is just not worth it.

- Wearing nice clothes – ahh, the comfort and ease of pyjamas! If you're ever stuck on what to get a sick person for their birthday or Christmas, then PJs are a safe bet. I never realised how much time and energy I spent wearing nice clothes. I know this might sound silly, but nice clothes require maintenance. Be careful where you sit, watch you don't tuck your skirt into your knickers. Are you sure you want to eat that when you're wearing your new, white top? Making sure your strappy top is not flashing a little bit of something extra.

- Make-up – no one sees me and I don't see anyone, therefore its application is superfluous.
- Hair – I used to do beautiful and elaborate things with my hair, but as we have established in points 1 and 3, it's just not worth it. So I brush it twice a day – what more do you want?…ok, once a day. Well, fine, maybe it's once every two days.
- Nail polish – it's become my new bugbear. You have to put it on, wait for it to dry, then it chips within a day or two and you have to take it off again. It's pointless – unless you have an annoying little sister who seems to think that vandalising your nails with bright colours will make you bright and chipper again… Her optimism is admirable and annoying.

I have a tightness in my stomach as I place my partially read book and a glass of water on the table in the kitchen. I've deliberately chosen this seat because even if the sun comes out it's still shrouded in shade, so I'm not blinded so much by the light; I can also see the clock from here so I know when a respectable amount of time has passed and I can hint for Logan to go. I'm not good at asking people to leave, no matter how tired I am, so I tend to make up an excuse like a phone consultation with the doctors' surgery whose number, inconsequentially, I know by heart.

I'm trying to remember what I've forgotten when I hear the old brass knocker against the door. Everything inside me wants to ignore it, but I go down the hall and answer the door anyway.

'Hi,' Logan says brightly, stepping into the hall and briefly hugging me.

'Come in,' I say leading him into the kitchen. My heart sinks a little when he goes to my chair.

'Oh, you were sitting here?' he asks, pausing.

The old me would laugh and say, 'It doesn't matter, sit where you want.'

But the sick me has to be different. 'Yeah, I was just reading my book before you arrived.'

I have to say he gets Brownie points for falling into my trap. Some people are oblivious to my territorial markers.

'Any good?' he asked, sitting in the seat opposite me.

I can't help but smile a little, another trick of the sick. There comes a time when you're so ill for so long that all interesting activities become impossible, which results in a shortage of things to say. Having the book there is handy for conversational purposes, which is another reason why I left it there. The water is for drinking and to further mark my territory. For some reason, having a beverage, even a cold one, seems to mark the spot as being mine far more than just a book does.

Our conversation about the book is short-lived, but that is all right because Logan is never short of things to say.

'Yeah, he's pretty much broken his back which means I'm going to be home until he's more mobile.'

'How many months did you have left?' I ask.

'Erm, about five. It's not a year of travelling like I'd planned, but never mind. I got a bit of my money back, so it could have been worse,' he says light-heartedly.

'Can your little brother not look after the farm, or has he already started uni?'

'No, he leaves at the end of summer like me but he's not the farming type. He's more...studious. Honestly, he's scared of lambs.' Logan laughs. 'Can't say I'm delighted to be back, but there was no one else.'

'Couldn't one of the people working on the farm take over for a while?'

'My dad doesn't trust them to run the farm. They're fine for working on it, but not running it. He doesn't trust them not to skim half off the top.'

I'm surprised when I look up at the clock and realise that Logan's been here for three hours. It doesn't feel like three hours and I don't even feel that bad. It's as though I've stolen some of his buoyant charisma, absorbing it through his presence. He has so many stories to tell about all the countries he's been to, and all the things he's done, and I find myself laughing at them – not the kind of laugh I had before but it's not forced the way it is with others; it comes more easily. I'm actually disappointed when he says he has to leave. I think he saw it on my face because as he disappeared off down the drive to his car, he shouted that he would be here for a while and threatened that next time he'll get me out of the house.

I'm barely back in my pyjamas when I hear a car pulling into the drive. I go to the window and sigh as I see my aunt's car. I have to admit I'm disappointed: I was hoping to rest a while before she came home. As I head to the kitchen I can hear her coming in the back door.

'Hi,' I say as I enter the kitchen.

'How are you?' my Aunt Beth asks, taking off her coat.

'Fine, thanks. You?'

'Yeah, I'm fine,' she says, sounding tired. She's quite slim, my

Aunt Beth, and roughly the same height as me. Her dark brown hair is tied back and her face is clear of make-up.

'How was work?' I ask, pulling out my chair and sitting on it because my legs are getting sore.

'It was fine. Busy this morning but it was quiet this afternoon, so I thought I'd come home early.'

And that's our entire evening's worth of conversation used up within seconds. Everything is fine – we're all fine – it has to be fine. Only, for once, I actually have something to add.

'Logan came round earlier,' I tell her hesitantly.

'And how is he?' Aunt Beth asks quickly, struggling to hide the surprise and excitement from her voice.

I fill her in on his news as we make the dinner. I've always liked my aunt's cottage. It's homey and it's just what a cottage should look like. It's an old black house really. It was a ruin before my aunt and uncle renovated and extended part of it. Not that you'd know that the new part we're currently standing in was new. My uncle's a joiner and my aunt an electrician, a match made in renovation heaven; it's just a shame their marriage wasn't. When our tea's ready we go to the sitting room to eat it. We have long since given up eating in the kitchen. It's far less painful with the TV to fill the void where conversation should be.

The hours pass and the programmes we watch change, but I stay the same. I don't move. I'm leaning against the arm of the chair with my head held up by a pillow. I keep telling myself to get up – it's only going to get worse, I have to move but I can't; I know what I'm feeling will mean and I don't want to face it. I don't want to endure it again.

There's this constant weight inside me as though my limbs, head and torso are filled with sand, so that no matter which position I'm in, the weight of it follows me. Every day I carry its weight but as the day goes on, as I use the little energy and strength I have, the weight becomes an unbearable burden. I can feel its different layers getting heavier, the deeper the sand becomes. Everything inside of me hurts, everything aches, burns and stings. It feels like something's gnawing through every millimetre of me, every tissue, cell, bone and organ, like woodworm devouring wood and leaving hundreds of tiny holes in its wake, until so much damage has been done that the wood disintegrates to dust. I'm afraid if I move, I will crumble.

I must move, though. I know I must, so I use the arm of the chair to help push me forwards to the edge of the seat and then I stop, tired and out of breath. Aunt Beth sees me and hastens to her feet. She stands beside me, her arms extended, ready to help me. I take a deep breath and heave myself upwards. I can feel my legs tremble under the pressure put upon them, my joints aching under the weight they can't support. Aunt Beth grabs me under my arm before my legs give way, and helps me upright.

This is the part of me the doctors don't see. The part they can't understand no matter how desperately I try to explain to them. I wish they would listen to me, I wish they would believe me, I wish just one of them would take the time to understand.

Although I'm the same height as my aunt, I now only come up to her shoulder because my back's so hunched over. I take a step – it's nothing more than a shuffle because the sand inside of me is pulling me downwards. I feel as though someone has replaced my insides with a very frail and infirm ninety-year-old. We reach the door of the sitting room and I cling to the wooden frame. I never understood until I was ill what a difference holding onto something could make: how the arms could relieve the pressure on the legs just by having something solid to cling onto.

'Do you need to go to the bathroom?' Aunt Beth asks.

'Yes,' I say. My voice is so weak it comes out as a whisper.

Aunt Beth has me under one arm and my other is outstretched, reaching for the long unit in the hall to hold onto as we shuffle towards the bathroom. My breathing's heavy from exertion as we reach it. My aunt undoes the button on my jeans and leaves me to it.

I sit for a long time, my arm resting on the cold bath beside the toilet, its coldness penetrating into my arm but it keeps me upright; it keeps me balanced. The wooden floor and tiled walls swim before my eyes. I resent each tear that follows. I can't get up, I've tried, that's why I'm holding onto the bath because without it I would be on the floor right now. They gave up on me, my legs, they gave up. I try to straighten my back to relieve some of the pressure but I don't have the strength to hold it there. I try to call for my aunt but my voice is so feeble I'm not sure she hears me, so I whistle; I hate doing it – it's disrespectful but it's so much easier than trying to shout. I wipe my face before she enters – I don't want her to see my tears.

In my dining room, she helps me onto the sofa bed. I try to lift my legs but I don't have the strength to lift them high enough, so my aunt has to lift my legs into bed for me.

'Do you need anything?' she asks, her voice cracking. I shake my head slowly. 'Ok.'

Aunt Beth reaches to turn off my lamp. She must have put it on when I was in the bathroom. Before she does, I catch her eye but I quickly look away because the raw pain I see in them cuts me to my core. I watch her darkened figure move to the door. She looks back at me, her outline dark against the bright light in the hall and then she leaves me, leaving the door open a little in the hope that she might hear me if I call.

I manage to pull myself onto my side; I'm about to close my eyes when I spot another pair watching me. The dog's head is resting on the bed in front of me, watching me eye to eye. He's about the size of a Labrador, although we don't really know what breed he is: a hairy one at any rate. When Dog was a puppy we took so long to find a name that he got so used to being called Dog we couldn't change it. With my hand that's resting on top of the covers I pat the bed feebly. I'm always amazed how he knows when I'm severely unwell. Normally he would leap onto my bed with such a force that I would feel as though I might be capsized off it, but he jumps up so gently that I can barely feel it. He curls himself into the shape of my body, his warmth my only comfort.

I'm not sure how much time passes. I just want to sleep. How can the body and mind be so exhausted but still sleep hides, lingering in the fringes of the darkness in my mind. Aunt Beth comes through and tells me that she's going to take Dog for his nightly run. It was something my aunt and I used to do together: I would go cycling alone with Dog in the morning, and my aunt would join us for our run at night. I wait until I hear the front door shut. I listen for her footsteps outside my window as she walks down the gravelled drive before my resolve breaks. I can't help it and I can't stop it. I slowly curl into a ball as the sobs shake my frail frame. My mouth is open and I'm certain that if I had the energy, then I would be screaming.

So I hope you understand now why I calculate, evaluate and deliberate the consequences of everything I do. That innocent cup of tea…do you see what a difficulty it could pose to me now? So I hope you understand, I hope you do see, that while I'm afraid I might die, I'm terrified to live.

Chapter Three

When I wake the next morning, I find myself lying on the very edge of my bed. I feel as though I'm pulling against elastic bands in order to open my reluctant eyes. When I look at the clock on the unit beside my bed it reads that it is three in the afternoon. I try to move away from the edge of the bed, but something is shoved up against my back. I strain my neck trying to see what it is, only to find a hairy mass at my back. It takes me a moment to figure out what it is.

'Dog,' I mutter sleepily, fighting to keep my eyes open.

He lifts his head to look at me and then drops his head lazily onto my pillow. I feel as though my brain's been filled with cotton, preventing the electrical impulses and messages from travelling properly, leaving me disorientated and dazed as I gaze about my room. And not for the first time I wonder if this is what it feels like to wake up when you've been comatose and heavily medicated for days or even weeks. I don't feel as though I've slept for the best part of seventeen hours: it feels more like one. I always feel that way when I wake, though, as if I've not slept at all. 'So you don't feel you get any benefit from sleeping – you're just as tired when you wake?' the doctors would say. Now I'm becoming more awake I'm growing increasingly aware of how uncomfortable I am. With a sigh of resignation, I heave myself out of bed and look at the tiny sliver of space I had to sleep in, while Dog had the rest of the bed entirely to himself, to stretch luxuriously across, and yet he still squashed himself against my back.

It takes three cups of tea, an hour and a half, and a bowl of cereal to get myself awake fully. I've figured out a method of doing things. It's not exactly foolproof – it's time-consuming and frustrating, but it does get things done. So once I'm functioning, I begin to clean the kitchen. I rest for half an hour to recover from the exertion and then I hang out the washing and rest once again because all that stretching comes with its own unique set of aches and pains. I know I should be spending the day in bed but I can't help it: it's my default setting from when I was a child.

When my little sister and I first came to live with my aunt I was hounded by guilt and disposability, so my seven-year-old self did everything she could to be the opposite. As I grew older the guilt faded; I continued to do all the things I did before but I didn't do them out of guilt, I just did them to help out. But now I'm ill, the guilt of it hangs about my shoulders – it haunts me everywhere I go. I was so independent, so free. Now I'm a shackle tied to my aunt's leg, weighing and dragging everyone around me down. I'm not being pessimistic and I'm not feeling sorry for myself: it's simply a fact. And one I can't stand. It chips and tears away at you so I do what I can, when I can, however long it may take me. Besides, I hate being in bed with a vengeance – there are things to be done and an existence to endure. One complements the other because now my brain's ability to function has reduced so spectacularly, I can't think and work at the same time and thinking can be dangerous. I don't recommend it.

By the time evening comes I'm too tired to cook anything properly, so I just shove a pizza in the oven. I'm eating it at the kitchen table with my book in front of me when I feel something moving in my forehead. I lift my hand and place it over my forehead but after a moment, when nothing happens, I lower it. Seconds pass and I feel it again, I look up to the mirror on the far wall to see that my forehead is moving, just above my left eye. Something is moving beneath my skin, tugging at it between two points, going to and fro, like water in glass when it's rocked back and forth. I watch it with horror and fascination. The doctors always dismiss it – they like to focus on just a few symptoms as though the rest are irrelevant in finding out what's wrong with me. Sometimes I wonder if they're stupid or if I'm complex: for most doctors I meet, I come to the former conclusion.

It's after nine before my aunt comes home. I meet her at the back door where she comes in with her fingers entwined in plastic shopping bags and drops them onto the kitchen table.

'What's wrong?' my Aunt Beth asks, noticing me staring at the bags.

'Nothing,' I say quickly.

I hadn't factored in a food shop to my carefully planned and scheduled day and my aunt's not even finished – she's heading back outside for the rest.

I begin unpacking the bags, watching as each trip outside from my aunt brings more bags to be unpacked.

'Your dinner's still warm if you want to get it, I'll unpack these,' I say as my aunt shuts the back door.

'You sure?' Beth asks uncertainly.

'Yeah, I had a quiet day,' I say and it's true: by anyone else's standards, it was.

'I got your shampoo,' she says, opening the oven and taking out her plate with the oven gloves, adding with concern, 'I couldn't get the one you asked for but a woman in the shop said it was just as good. I can take it back?'

I spot the bottle sticking out of one of the many bags on the table. I pull it out and look at it. It's not the one I wanted – it's not the one I asked for – I have to admit I'm disappointed.

'Yeah, thank you,' I say with a smile because I know that's what she wants and she looks relieved when I do.

As soon as she leaves the room I set the bottle aside. I wrap my arms around me, a laden feeling in my stomach; it's just one more thing on an already dangerously high pile of things. You can't get annoyed with the person who's doing you a favour... and that's what it is, another thing to add onto my painfully long list of things I feel indebted to her for. I know she tries. It's not as if she chose the wrong one on purpose. What's she supposed to do – phone me up each time she can't get the one I asked for and go through every single bottle in the shop so I can pick an alternative?

I resume unpacking the bags, shutting the cupboard doors with more force than I'd intended, the noise sharp in my ear, but it's a strangely satisfying little rebuke to my situation. I just wish I could go and get these things myself, like I always used to. I liked to go to the shops, I liked the sights, smells, noises, movement, colour. I liked it all. But I have to credit the internet with giving me a little of my independence back because I *can* buy things online, but because we live in the middle of nowhere the postage for everything is ridiculously high, which greatly limits what I can buy.

My aunt comes through to make herself a cup of tea just as I'm about done with the shopping. There's a wee pile on the table of her things, and a wee pile of mine, for each of us to take to our rooms.

'Joyce,' Aunt Beth asks in a bemused voice. 'Why is there a half-empty bottle of milk in the cupboard next to the tinned tomatoes?'

'Ehh, I don't know,' I say awkwardly. 'I'll put it in the freezer.'

'The fridge?' my aunt says, handing it out to me.

'Yeah, why?' I ask, taking the carton from her.

'You said freezer.'

'I meant the fridge,' I say, forcing myself to laugh to ease the worried expression on her face.

I open the fridge and busily begin reorganising its contents so that she won't see the fear on my face.

'Joy, what time are we leaving yours for Connor's party?' Rebecca asks.

We're in the lunch hall at school. I'm with Rebecca, Amy, Logan and Paul in the lunch queue which seems to be growing rather than shortening.

'Ehh, rabbit over the hare,' I say, trying to tell them what time we are leaving for Connor's.

The four of them burst out laughing; now I'm laughing, too, because what I've said is so ridiculous that it's funny...only a part of me is telling me it's not.

Word misplacement, I think that's what they call it. We all do it from time to time but mine is different. It happens more often than I would care to admit. Sometimes, I can hear the wrong words coming out as I say them, yet I'm powerless to stop it. Other times, like just now, I'm oblivious, until I see the strange expression on the face of my aunt or whoever I'm with. I often wonder what this illness, whatever it is, is doing to my brain. There are times when the words will get stuck all together. I go to say them, but then they're snatched from my mouth. It's stupid because I know what I'm trying to say, but it's as though I've forgotten how to form the words. At times I forget what I'm saying altogether: I'll be in the middle of a sentence and poof...it's gone and I'll be left in this awkward silence before I say jokingly, 'What was I talking about?' although I have to say it's even more embarrassing when the person can't tell you. Just goes to show what a scintillating conversationalist I am!

I go through to the sitting room and sit on the couch nearest the door. I like the draft, especially when the fire's on. My aunt's laptop is sitting on the couch next to me. I accidentally knock it as I shift around on the couch, trying to get comfortable. Its sleeping screen comes to life and reveals what my aunt was looking at: parathyroid disease. She has another tab open about ME/CFS (chronic fatigue syndrome) and another on MS (multiple sclerosis). I quickly put the laptop to the sleep setting: I don't want her to think that I was deliberately looking at it.

Joyce, have the doctors considered lupus? Hope you're feeling better. Aunt Beth said you've not been so good lately. I'll be home this weekend so we can curl up and watch DVDs, I'll do your nails! Thinking of you, big sis Xxx

I used to get messages all the time from my little sister Sarah and (although not as often) from my older cousin Kate, with ideas of what could be wrong with me. I don't get those messages so often now – the well of inspiration has run dry. There's nothing new to suggest. Still, my aunt hunts, hungry for answers, hoping for a cure…her desperation is something we share.

Aunt Beth comes through and hands me a cup of tea, she sits down but after ten minutes she has fallen asleep, her cup tipping ever closer towards her lap. As gently as I can, I uncurl her fingers from around the cup and place it on the coffee table in front of us. I'm not sure what makes me feel more lonely: being home on my own or being here with my sleeping aunt.

I have to sleep downstairs tonight. I think you know now what that means, but it's ok, it wasn't under such strong duress as before.

Chapter Four

Beth.

I look at my watch which tells me it's half-six and then I glance to the nearby window as though to confirm, by the quality of the light, that my watch is telling the truth. As I gather my tools from around the room which will soon be an office space, I realise that if I leave now, then I could make it home in time to have dinner with Joyce. I dump my tools into my bag, the clicking clatter they make as they land echoes in the empty room. I could send Joyce a message to wait for me, but my hand stays steadfastly by my side and instead I wander around the room, looking for any tools I missed or any jobs I could do that I overlooked. With a heavy sigh I return to my bag empty-handed and heave it onto my shoulders before heading to the stairwell. The lift's still under construction, which means I have to climb the five flights of stairs, but I quite like the delay it gives me. At the last flight of stairs, I pause to get my car keys from my jacket pocket. Tangled in the keyrings is a folded envelope with a list of food from my overdue food shop. I've been meaning to go all week, but it's been so busy at work that I've not had a chance to. It can wait until the weekend, I tell myself, but then, if I go now I can spend the whole weekend with Joyce undisturbed. It's not fair for her to be alone all day, stuck in the cottage, I tell myself, but she's not alone, another part of me reminds…she has Dog. I walk down the last flight of stairs with a newfound bounce to my step. I truly don't know what I'd do without Dog – I never really wanted him, but it turns out he was the best purchase I've ever made.

***

I stroll around the huge supermarket with my trolley, perusing shelves like everyone else; its normality is soothingly nostalgic. It's quieter this time of night, which is another good reason to go shopping now, I reaffirm to myself. I head down the cosmetics aisle until I reach the shampoos, conditioners and body washes, where I stop to quickly search for the one on the list. The entire list has been written by Joyce and it's her shampoo and conditioner I'm hunting for now. The range of choice is baffling, the bright colours and different shapes all pulling at my attention. Unable to find the one on the list, I grab the nearest bottle and put it in the trolley. I head down the aisle but pause at the end of it, my insides uneasy: she's only asking for a bottle of shampoo: surely I can get her that much.

I go back to the array of shampoos and this time I pay attention to the labels…but still I can't find it. I begin moving bottles onto the floor to see if it could be behind them; I even begin pulling out the boxes at the back to see if it's there, my breathing quickening in my frantic desire to find the right one. It's all Joyce has asked from me, surely I can do this, this one simple thing. I brush my brown hair away from my face as the boxes from the back of the shelves start piling up around my feet.

'Can I help you?' a man asks with a disapproving tone.

I look up from my crouched position to find a young man

wearing the shop's uniform and a name tag to inform me he's called 'Toby'. My dad had a cat called Toby, I think dazedly.

'Erm, yes. I'm looking for this,' I say, showing him the name of the shampoo on the list.

'If it's not there, we don't have it,' he says shortly, looking pointedly at the mess I've made on the floor before turning and walking away.

'Excuse me,' I say more loudly than intended. 'Can you check your storeroom please?'

'If it's not there, we don't have it,' he replies.

'I need this shampoo. I-I.' I glance self-consciously around me, suddenly aware of the people who have stopped to look at the commotion before adding more calmly, 'My niece is ill, she needs this shampoo.'

'Oh, ehh, wait here,' the man says awkwardly, quickly striding off down the aisle.

I shift nervously from foot to foot – I'm not convinced he will come back without security. While I wait, I put all the boxes back on the shelves, my embarrassment sinking deeper into my core as I put back each box and bottle.

'We don't have it,' the guy says a few minutes later, holding out another bottle of shampoo. 'The woman I asked said that this one was really good, though.'

'Thanks,' I say, unable to meet his eyes for my own embarrassment. Taking it from him, I examine the bottle with both relief and disappointment.

I finish the rest of my shopping as quickly as possible, while trying to avoid the young shop assistant as he moves about the store with a trolley full of things to be stacked on the shelves. After I pay, I head to the little café near the entrance of the shop.

The café is shut but you can buy a takeaway cup of tea from a machine in the corner. I sit with my trolley at one of the many empty tables and sip my scalding hot and rather flavourless tea. I know I should go home but the idea of returning to that bleak and miserable house fills me with dread. It used to be such a happy wee place. I'd come home and the kids would often be playing in the garden, laughing and smiling or they would be sitting at the kitchen table, mocking each other as they did their homework. It was a home full of happy noises...of course it wasn't always that way, in fact, but that's the way I like to remember it. There's nothing happy about it now, it's a place of darkness – literally and figuratively. With the curtains drawn the house feels oppressive and trapping. It's not so bad in the winter months when the long nights were pleasing to cover over with bright, cheerful patterned curtains, but now the evening sun shines through them and the walls of the house no longer feel cosy; instead, they're claustrophobic.

I watch the steam rise up from my paper cup, the laughter of a young couple walking past the empty coffee shop catching my attention. They pause beside a stand full of sunglasses, each of them taking it in turns to try a pair on. They look like they're preparing for a holiday: with suncream and flip-flops sticking out from their basket. I envy them, their future is full of bright things and their present is full of smiles and anticipation because they know, they know their future is full of wonders. I wonder when I lost that. When I lost the ability to see any hope. I can't see any end to this disaster which does not entail more. I used to be full of dreams, ideas and hopes for the future. I was going to travel once the kids left home, take classes and workshops, I was going to do and see things I'd never done before – the possibilities were endless once you started to explore what was out there. I often see Joyce watch the people around us as I am now, on the odd occasions that we go out, and she gazes at them with such longing, with such a hunger and a desire to live it's like it physically hurts her to see what she should be and what she now no longer is. I understand why she doesn't like to leave the house but it's smothering her being there all the time. She barely used to be in the house before she was ill – she was always out doing things: walking, cycling, running or simply being out with her friends. Now there's no escaping the shadow which haunts the very air I breathe. It doesn't matter if we're in the same room or not, her illness still haunts the space between us, it's like she's the living ghost of someone long dead, the memory of them everywhere and nowhere all at the same time.

I watch the couple until they move out of sight and an older woman with far more vigour than Joyce takes their place within my view. I wonder, when Joyce leaves the house, if there is anything she can gaze upon without envy and without pain. She never says it, but I know she feels it. I lift my paper cup to my lips but pause, the grey, flavourless and now cool substance so unappealing that I get up and drop the cup in a nearby bin and head out of the shop, its sanctuary no longer satisfying.

It's dark when I pull up to the cottage and park round the back. The lights from within the cottage glow through the shut curtains, creating an outward illusion of homeliness, yet there's still something uninviting and unfriendly.

I don't allow myself to dawdle as I turn off the engine and gather up my things: if I do, I'll never be able to make myself go inside. Joyce is waiting for me inside the back door. She looks tired and her arms are wrapped around herself anxiously – she's always so anxious these days. I drop the heavy shopping bags onto the table, my fingers throbbing from the plastic cutting into them.

'What's wrong?' I ask.

'Nothing,' Joyce says quickly. She moves stiffly to the table and begins to unpack the bags.

I hesitate before going outside to get the rest.

'Your dinner's still warm if you want to get, I'll unpack these,' Joyce says as I shut the back door with my foot, my hands overloaded with bags.

'You sure?' I ask with uncertainty. I hadn't realised till now how tired and hungry I was.

'Yeah, I had a quiet day,' Joyce says and I hope it's true because she was exhausted yesterday.

'I got your shampoo,' I say nervously, opening the oven and taking out the plate with the oven gloves, adding with concern, 'I couldn't get the one you asked for but a woman in the shop said it was just as good. I can take it back?'

Joyce sees the bottle inside one of the many bags on the table. She pulls it out and looks at it. I feel myself freeze with my hot plate in my oven gloved hands: waiting for her reaction.

'Thank you,' Joyce says with a smile that doesn't reach her eyes. I smile back, my muscles relaxing – I'm relieved she's happy with it.

I head to the sitting room and sit on the couch, my dinner balanced on my lap. The TV's already on and I turn up the volume to drown out the banging of the cupboard doors as Joyce puts away the shopping. After a second I turn it back down and listen with pleasure as Joyce bangs about the place; it makes me smile because her hearing must not be too sensitive today but my smile fades as I think over how unwell she was last night. As soon as I finish my dinner I turn on my laptop and start my mandatory search of illnesses.

After a while I get up and head to the kitchen where Joyce is still unpacking. I consider helping her, but I'm eager to return to my laptop – I've just found a new illness which could be Joyce. It's taking longer and longer to find new illnesses which match her symptoms. In a way it makes it harder, knowing that the pool in which I fish is getting smaller, but in other ways it's more intoxication because surely, after two years of obsessively hunting, I must be close. As I wait for the kettle to boil I go to the cupboard to get myself a biscuit but my eye is instantly drawn to the white mass which is a carton of milk.

'Joyce,' I ask in bemusement. 'Why is there a half-empty bottle of milk in the cupboard next to the tinned tomatoes?'

'Ehh, I don't know,' Joyce says, coming towards me, her face pale and her eyes downcast. 'I'll put it in the freezer.'

'The fridge?' I say with a hard knot in my stomach, handing it out to her.

'Yeah, why?' she asks, taking the carton from me.

'You said freezer.'

'I meant the fridge,' she says with a laugh. I'm glad she can laugh because the increasing frequency of these mental mistakes is scaring me.

Chapter Five

The four main types of day for a chronically ill person:

- The good day – a rare to very rare occurrence in which the person feels better within themselves than they **normally** would. A good day is often marked by a reduced amount of pain, fewer feelings of fatigue and more mental awareness. Mobility is better but still restricted.

- The average day – is not always referred to by the amount of time it's experienced but by the pain, exhaustion, fatigue and mental dullness being of an average strength. Mobility is largely restricted.

- The bad day – equals being bedbound. Its effects can be felt from the moment of awakening or at some point during the day. Bad days can occur as often or more often than average days. A good or average day can slide into being a bad day with abrupt quickness or as the result of exertion. Pain very strong. Mobility is greatly impaired.

- The toxic day – the person is dependent on the people near them for every basic need, including feeding. Pain intolerable. Mobility is near non-existent.

Of course there are many in-betweens – one can slide between the fringes of 1 and 4 throughout the day. Exertion and resting: it's a dance on the dangerous line that divides them.

There's something so much more satisfying about waking upstairs in your own bed. Perhaps it's because I know this room is mine, well, really it's my aunt's but I have a claim to it that's far stronger than I have to the dining room. I'm not an imposter in this room, with its peach and cream walls which I painted when I was thirteen. I always liked this room, mainly because of the large window whose cushioned seat looks out over the fields, forest and mountains. I wasn't exaggerating when I said that we lived in the middle of nowhere, way out in the back of beyond, where people think you're either mad or brave if you don't have a 4x4 for the winter. It's the kind of place where people wave when they pass one another and where people stop to offer you a lift if they think you need one. I didn't always live in a place as friendly as this. Before my parents died in a car crash when I was seven, I used to live in a built-up area; I don't remember it being particularly rough but if someone had stopped and offered me a lift I would have legged it in the opposite direction.

I glance behind me at the door, thinking that I can hear Dog outside it, but after a moment of silence I turn back around. There used to be pictures all over my door and wardrobe, of my friends and me, at school, parties, trips away. But I took them all down a few months after I had to drop out of school and I came to the realisation that I would never see most of them again. I won't lie…it hurt. People I had known for six years just dropped me when they realised I couldn't do any of the things I used to. Some kept in touch by text until they left for university. After that, I was just someone they had known from their past and that's where I've been ever since, in every sense of the word. So I took their frozen happy faces down, theirs and my own. I couldn't stand to have them watching me, jeering and mocking me. I couldn't stand to see the contrast with the girl I was once and everything I'd lost. Now my room is devoid of reminders. I have them stuffed in a box in my wardrobe. I went a little frantic in doing so, grabbing everything that held any meaning to the old me and hiding it away. That person is gone now; she's dead. I miss her and I grieve for her. My body is her vacant shell, clinging onto the remnants of a life I can't bear to remember.

My phone beeps beside me on my desk. When I look at the screen I can see it's from Logan: *You free on Friday?*.....and my deliberating starts all over again! If you think it's frustrating, then you should try and be me. I put my phone down and continue reading my book. I have a pile of them to get through. I don't want to waste the time in which I'm sick, which is a difficult thing not to do, but when I'm feeling able I read the textbooks I bought and make notes to help me remember. I like to think I'm learning but if I'm being honest I don't remember most of what I've read.

My logic was sound. When I was first misdiagnosed I was told I would get better in six weeks. When that failed to happen I was told to go away and come back in six months if I was still "poorly". It was obvious by then that I wasn't going to finish the school year or be able to sit my exams. No exams, no university – so I thought if I studied I could get a head start on the college courses I'd applied for but I had to cancel them, too. Why universities and colleges have to send you rejection letters when you've cancelled your own application is beyond me. I can assure them that the extra twist of the knife was not necessary. I'm agonisingly aware of the future I've lost. I have felt first-hand every step of my debilitation and as all the things and activities which defined who I was were taken from me, one by painful one.

But still I sit here and study when I can in the hope that if I ever get better I might still be able to go to university. Hope is both my saviour and my enemy. It's my driving force, despite its cruel and crushing consequences when it's tossed so easily aside by the reality of my illness.

Just one more lesson, that's all I have to get through and then school's done and I can go home, just one more lesson.

I'm sitting at a table which I share with five others in my English class. The room's quiet except for the loud sound of pens inking their owners' paper as they write and the odd rustle as people turn the pages of their books and shift about in their chairs. I glance over at Connor's jotter and my heart plummets. He's on the last question and when I look over at the other people on the table they're nearing the end, too.

I try to covertly rub my neck and shoulders; the pain in them has been building since break this morning. My head hurts. It feels as though my brain is swelling against my skull and the pain in the joints of my knees is becoming unbearable. I just need to get through today – don't worry about tomorrow – just get through today. I look down at my textbook and once again I try to read the words like I have been doing for the past thirty minutes. I notice that Connor's finished and he's reading the next chapter just for something to do. I'm still on the first sentence of the first page. I keep reading the same sentence but each time I get to the end I've forgotten what the start of it says. Over and over again I read it, each time with more desperation but I just can't remember. I force myself to continue reading the rest of the paragraph but the words are just bouncing off my mind. Those strong and upstanding letters become more meaningless by the moment. I look up at the clock, its ticking growing louder by the second – forty minutes have passed. I can't focus for all the noise, tick, scratch, rustle, tick. I'm so tired the letters are swimming before my eyes. Fifty minutes.

'All right, pack up your things. Anyone who's not finished the questions

in chapter five can do them as homework. Joy, can I have a word with you?'

I stuff my books in my bag and head over to Mrs Shallow's desk.

'I think you should drop out of the class,' she says with brutal bluntness. 'I don't see why I should teach someone who's not putting in the effort.'

I'm pretty sure she's not allowed to say that to a pupil but then, when have any of the teachers here cared about that?

'I am putting in the effort. I study for hours every evening,' I protest indignantly, as the school bell sounds.

Not putting in the effort! I'm standing here. Don't you know what an effort that is. I'm here five days a week. She knows I've been ill; she knows.

'I doubt that. I certainly can't see any evidence of it in your work, whereas I can in other people's,' Mrs Shallow says sanctimoniously, sitting back in her chair as though she's enjoying herself as the rest of the class begin to leave the room.

I wish I could think of something smart to say, something to outwit her. I used to be good at that but my brain's not like that anymore. She dismisses me with a flick of her hand as if I'm an annoying fly.

I almost missed my stop on the school bus: Amy had to shake me awake and shout to the driver to wait for me to get off. I fell asleep for a few hours when I came home but now I'm sitting at my desk with my English workbooks, doing the studying I apparently never do. I'm quite pleased with how much I've done. When I finish I pack my books back into my bag ready for tomorrow. I zip up my bag and then freeze…I can't remember anything I've just spent hours studying, I can't even tell you what subject I've studied.

I sigh and put down my pen. I can't concentrate now I've been distracted by Logan's message. I want to say yes to seeing him on Friday. It's been a few weeks since I last saw him, but the crime never outweighs the punishment. Nonetheless, I send a message back saying yes, because even when I bow to my illness it still punishes my submission. At least this way I feel I've done something to deserve it.

***

I'm getting ready for Logan's arrival. I actually feel relatively good. I'm slightly scared to say it, but I think I might be having a good day. My pain's not bad, the headache I've had for the past three days is gone. I'm not nauseous. I'm even quite bright!

I'm getting the post from the front door when my phone beeps from inside my pocket – it's from Logan: *I'm really sorry I can't come over. James phoned in sick and we have a delivery coming, unless you want to come and help?*

'Great,' I say dismally to Dog who's watching me from the end of the hall. 'What am I supposed to say to that?'

After a long minute of uncertainty, I message back saying "ok". There's no point wasting my good day and there's no point trying to preserve it; it won't be here tomorrow – I've tried that tactic.

Logan: *I was joking but ok. I'll come pick you up.*

'Oh great, how am I going to get out of that?' I say ill-temperedly. I like to pretend that I'm speaking to the dog and not myself because it makes it marginally less sad. I don't do it very often but I take it as a good sign because usually I wouldn't have the energy to bother.

I don't rush to get ready. It will be a good thirty minutes before Logan gets here. I meander to the kitchen and sift through the post. There's one letter for me and I can tell just by the envelope that it's from the hospital. When I open it I find a date and time for my next appointment in two weeks. Generally, you have to wait a month between appointments, so its arrival isn't a surprise.

I take an empty bottle from the cupboard and fill it with water before rummaging around the kitchen for a breakfast bar which I shove in my jacket pocket. I like to have one handy when I go out in case I need the sugar boost. I'm messaging my aunt to tell her about the appointment and that I'm going to the farm with Logan (my way of warning her what she might be coming home to) just as the knocker on the door goes. I head down the hall with my jacket slung across my arm and my sunglasses on top of my head.

'Hey, you ready to go?' Logan asks as I open the door.

'Yeah. Why are you looking at me like that?' I say warily, grabbing the house key from my jacket pocket and locking the door behind me.

'I don't know…you look different somehow,' Logan says as we walk to his car.

'I'm having a good day,' I say brightly, the gravel crunching beneath our feet.

'Ah good. You're feeling better!' he says eagerly.

'Erm,' I mutter.

I find it so difficult trying to explain to people – they take anything positive I say and run with it. I don't know if it's because they're so eager for good news or because they just don't understand. Feeling better doesn't mean I don't feel bad; an improvement isn't lasting – it won't be there the next time we meet.

'No, it…it just means I don't feel as bad as I normally do,' I tell him as he opens the passenger door of his parents' jeep for me. He darts around to the other side of the jeep and jumps in. I kind of wish he'd stayed and given me a boost: I'm not exactly balanced at the best of times nowadays, never mind trying to climb into this towering contraption. I do manage it, but with some rather ungraceful manoeuvres.

'You not going to shut the door?' Logan asks.

'Well, I never opened it,' I say shortly.

He stares at me for a moment before a smile creeps across his face. 'You can't reach the handle without climbing back out, can you?' he says, trying not to laugh.

'I…no,' I say ruefully.

He jumps out and comes round to the passenger side.

'It's not funny,' I tell him, but the smile on his face as he shuts the door makes it hard to resist one of my own.

Chapter Six

We stop at the side of one of the five large barns and outbuildings. There are fields all around us and I know from the other times I've been here that the house is nearby.

'Are you ok for opening the door?' Logan asks jovially.

'Yes,' I say dryly, trying not to smile.

When I open the door the smell of dung, straw and animal wafts towards me in the afternoon breeze which carries a mass of heavy and dark cloud towards us. I used to hate the smell of farms when I first came to live here. My little sister and I used to run past the farms with our breaths held. For years, the farmer would fertilise the fields around the cottage with slurry (which is basically fermented manure). The place would stink; you could smell it in the cottage – you couldn't hang your washing out to dry because when you took it in the clothes stank of it. It was so strong you'd have to put the clothes through the wash twice to get the smell out. But now the smells of a farm are strangely comforting. They remind me of when my little sister, cousin and I used to play in the fields and ride our bikes for miles down the road.

I follow Logan towards the nearest of the stone outbuildings, its roof made of corrugated iron. The closer we get to the large, wooden doors, the more nervous I become. I can feel myself tensing as the sound of movement and talking comes from within. I never realised there would be more than just us. I don't like this. I don't know what's going on. How can I calculate and minimise the consequences if I don't know what's going to happen? Sick people don't like surprises; we like to have all the information. We're not control freaks – we're just slaves to our illness and chained by its limitations.

'Oh, it's all right, Logan's here and he's brought reinforcement,' says a man in his mid-sixties, appearing from around the side of the door. His face is heavily weather-lined and covered with a day or more's worth of grey stubble. 'I'll speak to you later, yup, yup, aye see you then.'

I wrap my arms around me, the man's comment about Logan bringing reinforcement making me nervous. It's times like these that I wish my illness was obvious or that I could be more forthcoming about it, but people and doctors see me standing before them and they just don't see what I feel. I'm not sure what Logan thinks I'm capable of doing. I know by the comments he sometimes makes that he thinks I'm capable of doing more than I can.

The man hangs up the phone and comes towards us.

'Your dad said the driver's been on the phone and is just minutes away.'

'Good. How's James and his hangover?' Logan asks with a bitter edge.

'Ha!' The man barks a laugh. His face is round and jovial; his hair is thinning and going grey at the sides. 'I'm sure he's nursing his hangover with little pride.'

'Hmm,' Logan murmurs over the sound of the approaching lorry.

'Anyone would think he was upset about losing his first day

off in two weeks,' the man says to me as Logan steps out of the barn to direct the lorry to the right building. 'I'm Davey.'

'Oh yeah, sorry. Davey, this is Joy,' Logan calls to us, before adding to me, 'Davey's my uncle.'

'Hi,' I say with a small smile.

The sound of the truck is deafening. I wish I'd thought to take my earplugs, but before long the engine is turned off and the driver and another man jump out.

'What should I do?' I ask Logan hesitantly.

'Ehh…you could count the bags to make sure we have the right number,' he says, going into his pocket and pulling out a sheet of paper – with the order written on it – along with a pen. 'Last time they gave us twenty less than we paid for.'

The two lorry drivers begin chucking the bags of feed down to Logan and Davey, who in turn carry them into the barn to the only corner of clear space. The other end of the building is taken up with stacks of hay which almost reach to the roof.

Each time a bag is brought in, I check the brand and mark it off against the chart I made for myself on the back of the paper, but after less than ten minutes I can feel myself struggling against the strain on my knees and lower back. So I try moving about a bit to ease the pain.

'Logan, get the girl a bale to sit on,' Davey says, heaving a bag across his shoulder.

'Sorry, you should have said,' Logan says as he passes me. He grabs a square bale off a smaller stack and puts it down beside me. 'Don't sit down, I'm going to get another one so it's higher.'

'You making her a throne, Logan.' The lorry driver laughs almost snidely, chucking a bag down to Davey. 'I thought all that feminist nonsense meant woman had to work.'

Logan glances at me, but I can't meet his gaze – my insides are cold. Everywhere I go people make assumptions, closed, narrow-minded judgments based on their own experience because they're too ignorant to learn anything beyond it. Why is she not at school?...must be skiving. Why is she walking with a stick?... oh I know, she must have injured her leg – because, of course, that's the only explanation for why a young person would need a stick; it couldn't possibly be anything else. Why is she not helping with the bags?...she must be lazy or, according to this apparently misogynistic man, I'm a delicate woman who's happy to use her right to vote but not to get off her arse and help the wage earner.

'Someone has to make sure you're not stealing off us,' Logan says humorously, but there's an undercurrent in his voice that pulls the lorry driver up short.

It takes an hour to unload the lorry. I had to shift my haystack three times as the mound grew. I was quite pleased with myself that I managed to move them on my own, that was until I saw the lorry driver smirking at me. Once they finish, Logan disappears off to get their money. Davey's chatting to the other guy as the lorry driver comes up to me.

'Your receipt, dear,' he says, handing me a piece of paper.

'I'm chronically ill,' I say meekly, my heart hammering in my chest as I take the receipt from him. It's the best my brain can come up with right now. Perhaps I should have ignored him, but him calling me 'dear' was something the old me couldn't let slide. The old me put people like him in their places; she corrected their blind ignorance; she had the intelligence and quick-wittedness to do so.

'Oh, right,' the man says awkwardly. He looks from me to the hay bales I'm sitting on. I can practically see the connection dawning slowly on his face. 'Right, well…I'm sorry.' At least he has the decency to look ashamed as he turns and heads back to his lorry in time to meet Logan who gives the man his financial dues.

'Are you ok?' Davey asks, giving me a strange look.

'I'm fine,' I say a little breathlessly, my hands holding tightly to the outsides of my thighs. My comment to the lorry driver is leaving me as shaken as if I'd confronted an armed robber.

'I think we've earned ourselves a cup of tea!' Davey says happily, rubbing his hands together as Logan comes over.

'I can make it if you tell me where to go,' I say quickly over the rumble of the lorry's engine.

'I'll come with you,' Logan says.

'You need to mix the lambs' feed,' Davey reminds him. 'I'm sure Joy and I will manage.'

If I'm being honest I'd rather stay with Logan: I know where I am with him, whereas Davey is unknown and unmeasurable. I don't really feel I can say that, though, so I agree despite myself. When I stand up, I can feel myself sway a little before I find my balance.

'Here, you can give an old man with tired arms some support,' Davey suggests, taking my hand and putting it through his arm the way my aunt does when I leave the house with her.

Logan gives me an amused look as Davey leads me out of the barn. As we walk across to one of the other barns, I get the feeling that I'm the one who's getting the support rather than Davey. We go through a red door at the side of one of the barns which leads into an office. There's a door at the other end of it which presumably leads into the barn. The walls and roof are made of plyboard, and there's a sink and mini-fridge in the corner opposite the desk and cabinets.

'You have a seat,' Davey suggests, taking the kettle from its holder on the desk and going to the sink.

I pretend not to hear him. I don't want to let him make our drinks when he's the one who's been working, so I take three cups from the tray beside the kettle and start adding tea bags into the heavily stained cups. I add three teaspoons of sugar into mine and half a teaspoon into Logan's. I don't normally take sugar but I still feel a little shaky after my comment to the lorry driver. While Davey still has his back turned to me, I pick my mug up and have a feel inside. I'm pretty sure they're clean, albeit displeasing to look at. I sit in one of the chairs while we wait for the kettle to boil. For a long time it doesn't seem to do anything, but then a small rumble begins to fill the room.

'Ahh, that's better,' Davey says, sighing as he sits in one of the other chairs.

'I never put any sugar in your cup, I wasn't sure if you took any,' I say to fill the silence.

'Oh, that's all right. I'm trying to cut back,' he says, subconsciously rubbing his relatively flat stomach. He looks at me calculatingly before saying with a measured lightness, 'Logan talks about you. He says you've not been keeping well…'

His sentence hangs in the air, waiting for me to dismiss or add to it.

'Yeah,' I say awkwardly, running my finger over the rough plastic of the chair's arm. 'They're not sure what it is yet.'

'Logan was saying you get tired a lot and you get aches and pains.'

A rather huge understatement but Logan can't be blamed, I remind myself, when I'm the one who's refused to say any more.

'Yes,' I say over the growing noise of the kettle.

'I hope you don't mind but I was watching you earlier...' Davey hesitates as though testing for my response, when I don't give one he continues. '...Have they tested you for Lyme disease?'

'I'm not sure,' I say, my stomach tensed but still squirming. 'I don't remember them saying anything about it.'

'You should make sure they test you. The way you move is so similar to my Alice....it was Lyme that she had,' he says, his voice growing thick and gravel-like.

'I will,' I say, taken aback. He runs his hand over his unshaven face as Logan appears through the door with what looks like three large baby bottles.

'Lambs?' I say questioningly as the kettle stops with a loud click.

'Well, it's not for us to drink,' he says jokingly. 'Have you fed lambs before?'

'Of course I have,' I say with mock indignation.

'You want to feed three more?'

We make up our tea and then pour it into two cup-sized flasks.

'Take the car, Logan,' Davey says as we're heading out of the door.

'They're just over there,' Logan says.

'I know but take it anyway,' Davey says heavily.

I give a rather awkward wave to Davey as we leave the office and head to the jeep. Logan opens the door and waits for me to get in this time before shutting it. The field we stop beside is just a few minutes' walk away but I'm glad Davey told Logan to take the jeep because it's all uphill.

We get out and I follow Logan to the nearest gate which he

opens and then shuts behind me. He takes the flasks from me and sits them on the gatepost. The huge field looks deserted but it's hard to tell with the contours of the land.

'MOLLY, DAISY,' Logan yells. He half-glances at me before yelling again, 'MISSES BAAA BA BELL!'

I snort, I can't help it. I was trying not to laugh.

'Look, I didn't name them,' Logan says, red patches spreading across his cheeks as three white blobs appear over the hill, racing comically towards us as fast as their little legs will carry them.

'Here,' he says, holding out one of the bottles for me to take from him.

The three lambs nearly collide into us in their haste. They instantly start jostling each other for prime position. I take the head of the nearest lamb and direct it towards the bottle in my hand. The mildly warm milk inside the bottle warms my cold fingers as the lamb drinks thirstily.

'I forgot how strong they are,' I say, clinging onto the bottle as the lamb tries to tear it from my hands like a game of tug-of-war. I'm glad it's Logan's who's feeding two at the same time and not me.

'It's the mothers I feel sorry for,' Logan says.

'Which one am I feeding?'

'Ehh, I think that's Daisy,' Logan says.

I tip the bottle higher as the milk disappears to try and stop the lamb from swallowing air. Once there's nothing left they clamber about Logan and me, nearly knocking me off my feet as one of them pushes in between my legs. I run my hand over their thick fleeces which are soft and slightly oily, the hair on their heads coarse and short, the contours of their skulls sharp against my fingers. After a while they grow bored, their hope for more food fading, and they wander off.

Logan walks a short way to the fence post where he left the flasks of tea. He hands me mine and then sits down on the rich, green grass. I hesitate – getting up off the ground is not really my best skill anymore, but it's not as if there's anywhere else for me to sit.

'They're pretty big,' I say, looking to the lambs which are meandering across the field.

'Yeah, I'm weaning them off the milk so it won't be long before I can stop feeding them,' he says, drinking from his flask. 'Anyway, how are you? Any news from the doctors?'

'I have an appointment in two weeks,' I say taking a sip from my flask, glad for the sweetness of my tea which seems to dance in my mouth.

'Could you not apply to go to college? You could do the exams you missed out on. It would give you something to look forward to,' he suggests, stretching his legs out in front of him.

'I wouldn't manage going into college each day,' I say awkwardly.

'You managed here ok,' he says, trying to be encouraging.

'That's one day. I don't get days like this very often,' I tell him, my heart picking up its pace within my chest.

'But even if you just did one subject–.'

'Logan….' I say in frustration but then I stop. It's not their fault they don't understand, but it's also not my fault that they're not prepared to listen.

'Sorry. I know you get tired and things, I just think it would be good,' he says gently, taking a long drink from his flask.

I brush my hand through the soft grass, the smell of earth pungent in my nose.

'I would if I could,' I say dismally.

'I know you would. I'm sorry,' he says fiddling with the top of his flask.

I'm pretty sure Logan thinks my mood is a bigger factor to my illness than my illness being the bigger factor to my mood. I will begrudgingly admit the power of positivity has a place, but positivity won't heal me…a diagnosis will. I finish the last of my tea as the rain which has threatened to fall all day suddenly does. Its heavy droplets follow us to the jeep with a growing force.

'You want to hang around for a bit?' Logan asks, his brown hair dripping and his shoulders soaked with rain.

'I should probably get home. I'm guessing you'll have a lot to catch up on.'

'Ha, yeah but it's fine,' he says, starting the jeep.

Chapter Seven

Five things the chronically ill would really like you, the healthy people, to do:

1. Make your own cup of tea – you may be the visitor but I'm the sick person you're visiting…so make your own beverage.

2. Arrive when you say you will – not three hours after when I'm no longer feeling well enough to see anyone. And by the way, it's just rude not to tell people you're going to be VERY late.

3. Will someone please give me a card? – I've been ill a long time now and I've not had a bag of grapes, a box of chocolates, flowers or even a Get Well card… hello, these are meant to be the rubbish perks you get for being ill.

4. Don't just see my illness – see me. I'm still in there, I'm just buried in the thorns of my disease.

5. Please don't turn up without warning – we don't like surprise visits. We're not normally well enough for them, and we may seem fine but your visit is going to harm us later.

I thought having a nap would help but when I wake later that evening, I feel awful. Physically I'm not too bad; well, when I say not too bad what I really mean is that I could be a lot worse. It was still bright when I went to bed after Logan dropped me off, but when I woke up it was to the dullness of dusk.

I head to the kitchen and make myself a cup of tea. I put the milk on the table but my aim is wrong and the carton falls off the edge, sending the white liquid all over the floor. I get onto my hands and knees and try to soak it up with a towel. I feel as if I spend a lot of time on this hard, cold floor, cleaning up a continuous mess.

'You spilt some milk?' my aunt says, coming through the back door.

I don't trust myself to say anything so I simply nod. The floor is turning into a white and black blur for the tears which obscure my sight.

'Do you need another towel?' Aunt Beth asks.

I nod, but when nothing happens I conclude she hasn't heard so I say, 'Yes,' my voice breaking.

'Hey, what's wrong?' my aunt asks, rushing towards me and crouching by my side with the towel forgotten in her hand.

It's all too much; I can feel myself cracking and my brain's too exhausted to stop it. The spilt milk, my illness, the milk, Logan, the milk, the doctors, the milk: it's suffocating, overwhelming.

'I spilt the milk,' I splutter.

'We can clean it up. Don't cry over spilt milk,' she says consolingly.

'That's not funny,' I howl like a toddler, all sense of composure and dignity gone.

'Ahh no, I never meant it like that,' Aunt Beth flusters. 'Come here.'

My aunt grabs me and pulls me into her; she leans us back against the cupboard door and rocks me slightly from side to side, like a child.

'Well, Dog's happy,' Aunt Beth says softly, speaking to me like the oversized child I've been reduced to.

I look up and see Dog licking the remainder of the milk off the floor. The mature me says that that's disgusting, that I need to clean his slobber up, but the child I've become just cries silently because it's all too much.

I don't know how long we stay there. I mark the time by the growth of pain in my body. The aching and the stiffness are building to an agonising degree, but I don't dare move from the rare comfort of my aunt's warm arms. I can take the pain, I know I can, because I've felt far worse.

Aunt Beth squeezes my shoulder and says quietly, 'Why don't I make us some dinner?'

I nod and a second later she gets stiffly to her feet. Aunt Beth pulls out a chair and helps me up onto it.

'Do you want to go through?' she asks but I shake my head; I need a moment for the first wave of pain to subside.

Aunt Beth begins making our dinner; I watch as she pulls things out of the fridge and onto the worktop. As I watch her, I wonder what she had envisioned her life would be like when she was my age, what her dreams and ambitions had been. Whatever it was, it definitely wasn't this – it wasn't me or the life I've forced upon her.

I get slowly to my feet. I wince. I can't help it, I look quickly to Aunt Beth but it's all right, she isn't looking. I walk to the sitting room, my steps small and heavy. I curl up on the couch in the sitting room, with my shame and embarrassment for company.

***

I'm woken by knocking at the front door. I ignore it at first but then my eyes catch sight of the clock by my sofa bed. It's half-twelve in the afternoon which means it's probably the postie with a parcel of electrical parts for my aunt. I heave myself out of bed and stumble my way, bleary-eyed, to the front door.

'Logan?' I say questioningly, even though there can be no doubt that it's him.

'Hey,' he says, sounding relieved. 'Sorry, did I wake you?'

'Yes,' I say dazedly.

'I can't stay – I have heaps to catch up on but you left your jacket in the car. I thought I better drop it round when I was passing anyway.'

'Thanks,' I mutter, my words slurring. The light hurts my eyes. Logan's turning into a hazy blur and I can feel myself sway. I need to sit down. I think I'm going to faint.

I turn my back on Logan and hasten to the stairs. I fall rather than sit on the bottom few steps. I bend forwards, putting my head between my knees and take slow, even breaths to try and calm my heart which is hitting against my chest, demanding its turn for attention. I'm oblivious to Logan standing at the front door, stranded and forgotten until I hear his footsteps coming into the hall towards me. The next thing I know he's sitting beside me, his hand rubbing small circles on my back.

'Are you nauseous or dizzy?' he asks hesitantly. 'Joy?'

I don't answer him, I can't. I'm trying not to faint, I really don't want to faint. Slow, even breaths, I tell myself, in through the nose….out through the mouth….in….and….out, but my heart is unruly. It's not under my command and my slow breathing is making my heart beat faster to the point where I feel like I might choke on it. I grab onto the banister because I'm afraid I may topple forwards. I can feel myself swaying…or maybe it's just the distortion of my vision. Logan's wrapping something around my shoulders. I think it might be my jacket, but it's warm inside of it so it must be his. Eventually my heart does slow; my breathing evens its beats – its tantrum has subsided but it leaves me shaken and weak, my chest sore.

I lift my head, testing my dizziness. When nothing happens, I pull myself up using the banister. I can feel the warning signs of weakness setting in, warning me the weight of the sand inside me is growing like the rising tide of a river. I step down off the stairs, my legs trembling as all my weight moves onto one and then onto the other. I cling onto the banister for as long as I can reach and then I use the hall wall to help keep me upright. It's not too bad, I tell myself. Shuffling one foot in front of the other, I know I can make it to the sofa bed. Just take it slow, remember your heart. It's getting from the doorway to the bed that is the hard bit because there's nothing to help me stay upright and keep me balanced.

I reach the doorway of my dining room and step forwards on my own. I wobble unsteadily without the support of the wall; my arms hover feebly at my sides doing the little that they can to help me balance, but then my hand is taken in another's. Logan reaches his other arm around my shoulder and squeezes me tightly to him. I've never been helped in this way. It makes it harder to walk but he's taking so much of my weight that the release of the weight on my back is merciful. We make our way to the sofa bed and I heave my legs up onto it; Logan doesn't know like my aunt to lift them. I feel my skin scraping sharply across the metal framework as I drag my legs up while Logan pulls the covers over me.

'What should I do? Can I get you anything?' Logan asks. He's worried, unsure – I can tell by his voice.

'I'm fine. Please go,' I say feebly. I can't look at him, I can't.

'I can't leave you,' Logan says.

'Please go, please. I just need to sleep. Please go,' I say, my voice quiet in its beseeching.

'Ok,' he says gently.

He pats me awkwardly on the shoulder before he retreats from my room. I wish Dog was here. I miss his warmth. I bite my lip to try and stop myself from crying but it's crushing, all that work and effort, all the lengths I went to and it's now been rendered pointless…because Logan saw; he caught a glimpse of the monster within me.

When I wake next it's five in the evening. I feel better, stronger, albeit a little shaky. I reach for my secret stash of breakfast bars which I keep hidden for times like these. I eat it slowly, allowing the sugar to absorb the shakiness inside me before I get up and cautiously make my way to the kitchen. I make myself a cup of tea and head slowly back to my room. I pause outside the sitting room door. I'm sure I heard a voice. A second later, I hear it again. I open the door to find Logan sitting on the couch with the TV on, the volume so low that I'm sure he won't be able to make out a word that's being said.

'Hi,' he says, sitting forwards onto the edge of the couch. He looks unsure whether or not to get up. 'How are you feeling?'

'Better,' I say. 'Why are you here?'

'It didn't feel right to leave. I wanted to know you were ok.'

I pause uncertainly before sitting in the armchair; its legs are stronger than mine.

'Thank you,' I say without looking at him, a hollowness inside me.

'I'm sorry I came round without calling first,' he says, filling the awkward silence.

I'm not sure what to say so I nod.

'Why didn't you tell me how sick you are?'

'I did,' I reply meekly, still looking at the contents in my cup.

'You told me you have bad days where you have to stay in bed and that you can't get out of it, but I...I never knew it was like that.'

'It wasn't that bad,' I tell him quietly, cradling my warm cup in my cold hands. They're always cold nowadays. I wish they weren't.

'How can you say that, Joyce? You could barely walk.' He sounds pained, although I can tell he's trying not to be.

'Because I've been far worse, Logan,' I retort feebly, finally meeting his gaze, and his bright brown eyes look tainted as though darkened by what they've seen.

'Why didn't you tell me?' Logan urges, his hands holding onto the edge of the cushions on the couch.

'I tried to explain it...' I say hopelessly, my hands gripping increasingly tightly on my cup as I try to get the words out.

'You should have made me understand,' Logan says tersely.

'How was I meant to explain what you saw in a way that you'd believe? You were telling me yesterday that I should be going to college,' I say slowly so that I can get the words out correctly.

Logan puts his head in his hands for a moment before lifting his head and saying, 'But if I'd known I would have done things differently.'

'I tried but...none, well, none of you could see it or understand it,' I say, desperately pushing the words out when all they want to do is jam in my mouth.

'You should have made me understand,' Logan says again, sighing in frustration.

I glare into my cup, my vexation making the words that follow easier than it normally would be. 'You all change the subject...or if you do listen then you'll only listen so far. I can see it on your faces when you don't want to hear any more...you recoil from me, even though what I'm telling you is so tiny. You squirm in your seat and I see you look at the door as if you want to run through it, so I stop because I'm terrified of...' I break off as my brain catches up with my mouth and I realise what I've said. My stupid, stupid mouth.

Even now he doesn't ask me to fill in the sentence so I rephrase it. 'I don't want to lose the few friends I have left.'

'You're not going to lose your friends,' Logan dismisses.

'Really? So what happened to all the ones I had in school?' I question.

'I never meant them,' Logan says brazenly. 'I meant your real friends.'

'Yeah, well they saw something similar and I've not seen or heard from them in a year and a half, despite all their promises,' I tell him quietly as I watch the steam rise from my tea, its journey so smooth and rhythmic. 'I get that it's hard to listen to and see but...'

'...But you have to live it,' Logan finishes for me.

I simply nod.

'....I'm sorry,' he says quietly. 'I just wish I'd known.'

I sigh. 'I didn't want you to look at me like you are now,' I say heavy-heartedly, regretting the words as soon as they come out.

'How? How am I looking at you?' he asks almost nervously.

Like my family do, I think to myself; like it physically hurts you to be near me.

'It doesn't matter,' I tell him. I've already said too much. I can feel my barriers rising and I welcome their return.

'Joyce…' Logan begins but whatever he was going to say trails away.

'Even you're doing it now,' I say trying to sound light and humorous but it still comes out sad. 'Calling me Joyce: you've never called me that.'

'I never realised I was,' he says, running his hand through his brown hair and then flattening it all back down again.

'I don't think they do either. They sometimes call me Joy and then they look shocked like I might tell them off or something,' I tell him, taking a sip from my cup.

'Really?' Logan says with his eyebrows raised and a smile that doesn't reach its normal heights.

'Yeah,' I add with a brightness I don't feel. I guess there's no joy in what they see, no Joy in Joyce. I suppose to call me Joy seems like a mockery. I take a long drink from my cup to cover the silence which is so unusual between us. 'I'm sorry you had to spend the day here.'

'Are you kidding? This is the most peace and quiet I've had since I came home,' Logan says, returning to his brighter self. 'Are you ok, though?'

'I'm fine now…if you need to go—,' I say, letting my voice trail away.

'No, no it's fine,' he says squirming in his seat, his eyes glancing at the clock on the windowsill.

'I'm just going to spend the day in bed. I'm getting tired so I should probably…' My voice fades out again: I don't really know where I'm going with this sentence.

'You sure?' he asks, sitting forward as though about to stand up, but he pauses. He looks nervous about leaving. I wonder whether he's more worried about leaving me alone or the backlash if something happens if he does.

'It's fine, Logan,' I say with an accidental briskness.

He gets up and is opening the front door before I've even managed to get out of my seat.

'Your jacket,' I say quickly, noticing it lying on the stairs where it must have fallen from my shoulders when I stood up.

'Ah yeah,' he says, grabbing and putting it back on. 'Call me if you need me to come back.'

And with that, he's gone, without a hug, a word or a backwards glance. I tell myself he's busy and has other things on his mind, but the doubtful and dubious part of me says otherwise.

Chapter Eight

Logan.

I tap the door with the metal knocker before glancing at my watch. When no one comes to the door, I glance at the windows at the front of the house. All the curtains are closed but that doesn't mean much; they're always closed nowadays. I think it might have something to do with Joy's eyes, but I often wonder how much better she would feel if they were open and she were free from the gloom of them being shut.

I knock on the door again, only louder this time. I'd be tempted just to leave her jacket on the doorstep but it looks like it might rain. I knock one last time. I'm about to give up when the door opens.

'Logan?' Joy asks, looking dazed and confused.

'Hey,' I say, with relief which turns to unease. 'Sorry, did I wake you?'

'Yes,' she says, the word slow to come out. She looks smaller somehow, as though sleep's shrunken her and stolen some of her height.

'I can't stay – I have heaps to catch up on but you left your jacket in the car. I thought I better drop it round when I was passing anyway,' I explain, feeling bad for waking her. Having said that, it's the middle of the day.

'Thanks,' Joy mutters. Her words sound slurred like she's been on a drunken night out and she's glaring at me which I'm hoping is because of the light, rather than me waking her, because it makes her look quite fierce.

She sways in the doorway and I nearly laugh: maybe she has been drinking. But then she turns her back on me and nearly falls onto the bottom of the stairs. She puts her head between her legs. I'm not sure what to do. I just stand there in the doorway before my head returns to me. I go into the cottage and sit beside her, hesitantly putting my hand on her back and rubbing it in the same way my mum used to when I was ill.

'Are you nauseous or dizzy?' I ask with uncertainty. I've had enough dealings with my siblings to know it's probably one or the other. 'Joy?'

Joy doesn't answer me. I wonder if I should get a bucket in case she's sick, but I'm not sure where I would get one. I look upstairs towards her room, wondering if the bin that I know she has under her desk would work as a bucket.

'Joy,' I say again but I'm not sure if she hears me. Her chest is heaving under my unmoving hand and a cold fear strikes me that maybe she's having a heart attack. Now I've stopped rubbing her back I can feel how cold her skin is, even through her top. I take my jacket off and put it around her shoulders, knowing that it will be warmer than her unworn one which is lying on the stair next to me.

Joy lifts her head up slowly as though it's a great burden upon her neck. I'm not sure what to say or do, so I do nothing. She grips onto the banister and heaves herself up. There's something wrong with her movements. I don't know what is it – I can't put my finger on it, but it quickly becomes apparent that there's something very wrong as she steps down off the stairs and shuffles forwards, her hand still clinging onto the banister as though it's her life-raft.

When she's too far away to hold onto the banister she lets go while at the same time reaching for the wall as though she's done this a hundred times before. I sit and stare at her: I know I should be doing something but I'm paralysed by the horror of what's unfolding before me. Where is her strength, her vibrancy?....my great-granny's more mobile. I don't understand: she was fine yesterday. She was better than I've seen her in a while, a small spark of her old self. I watch as her feet shuffle forwards, slowly, carefully, as though she's made of thin glass that might shatter at any moment. She pauses at the door to the dining room and I hear her sigh as if she can't believe how much further there is still to go.

Her sigh sends a jolt through me and I hasten to my feet, reaching out for her as she steps into the room. A spike of fear lurches into my gut as she wobbles dangerously. I quickly grab her cold hand, her fingers like pliable icicles against my warm skin. I put my other hand around her shoulders and squeeze her into me. I realise then what's wrong with her movements beyond them being fragile – they're weakened and cumbersome, like she's weighted down with cement. Her back's hunched as though she's carrying bags of it around her neck. It's as though she carries inside of her the weight of someone ten times her slim frame. I want to lift her into my arms and carry her, but I don't think she would ever forgive me if I did, so I press her into my side. I want to take as much of her weight as I can and I think it helps, I hope it does; I'm really not sure.

When we reach the bed I stretch over her and pull the covers around her; she looks so pale and cold, her auburn hair standing out in stark contrast to her pallor.

'What should I do? Can I get you anything?' I ask. I can hear the concern in my voice but I hope she doesn't.

'I'm fine. Please go,' she says so quietly that I can barely hear her. She's staring blankly at the side of her bed.

The room's been transformed since the last time I was in it: the table gone, this sofa bed here in its place.

'I can't leave you,' I say, stricken.

'Please go, please. I just need to sleep. Please go,' she says pleadingly.

I've never heard her plead – the old Joy never needed to. I don't want to leave her. I'd rather sit on the floor by her bed but I don't want to upset her further. I feel like I've invaded something personal, a shameful secret she never wanted me to know. I've crossed into an intimacy she never wanted me to have with her.

'Ok,' I say, trying to be gentle, soothing.

I pat her on the shoulder; I don't know if it would be appropriate to hug her.

I cross the room and shut the door as quietly as I can behind me. The front door's still open and I pause on its threshold: beyond it is freedom; behind it, entrapment. What if I leave and something happens to her because I'm not here? What if she gets up to get something and falls? It will be my fault because I left. I rest my head on the door frame in frustration as I think. No, it doesn't feel right; I can't leave and I'm not sure I want to.

I shut the door and sit on the stairs for a while. I've never seen her so vulnerable. She would have loathed for me to see her like that, so ashamed, her pride bashed, her independence vanquished. I put my head in my hands as I realise I've just been thinking about her as though she were dead. She's still the same person, I tell myself…only she's not. Joy was so strong and athletic – she had this never-ending supply of energy. I remember when a group of us were staying over at a friend's. We'd been at a party and had been drinking. Everyone was exhausted and wanted to go to bed, but Joy was full of life. She rallied everyone into going for a walk at four in the morning. Her cousin Kate fell into a ditch and lay at the bottom for a good few minutes before she could stop herself laughing long enough to get up. The next day when everyone else was hung-over and lethargic, Joy was annoyingly full of life. I don't understand where that person's gone or how I was so completely oblivious to her departure.

After a while I get up and head into the sitting room. I phone and arrange for James to cover me, but I know my dad won't be happy – we're meant to be cutting back on James's hours. We just don't have the money to have him working full-time but what else can I do? I don't have Joyce's aunt's number and I've got no other way of contacting her.

A few hours later Joyce appears around the side of the sitting room door.

'Hi,' I say, sitting forward onto the edge of the couch and accidentally knocking the remote which turns off the TV. She doesn't even seem to notice. She looks better than before so I'm not sure if I should get up to help her. 'How are you feeling?'

'Better,' she says though there are dark marks under her eyes. 'Why are you here?'

'It didn't feel right to leave. I wanted to know you were ok.'

She moves to the armchair, her movements less constrained.

'Thank you,' she says, although I'm not sure what for.

'I'm sorry I came round without calling first,' I say into the awkward silence.

She simply nods; she can't seem to bring herself to look at me.

'Why didn't you tell me how sick you are?'

'I did,' she replies quietly.

'You told me you have bad days where you have to stay in bed and that you can't get out of it, but I...I never knew it was like that,' I say, struggling to find the right words.

'It wasn't that bad,' she tells me meekly, cradling her cup in her hands.

'How can you say that, Joyce? You could barely walk,' I say, trying to hide the angst in my voice.

'Because I've been far worse, Logan,' she says. I can't imagine how it could be worse but I believe her.

'Why didn't you tell me?' I ask, my hands subconsciously holding onto the edge of the cushions, desperate to understand how she's been ill for two years and I never knew how seriously.

'I tried to explain it,' she says feebly.

'You should have made me understand,' I say tersely. I'm not sure who I'm annoyed at: her or myself.

'How was I meant to explain what you saw in a way that you'd believe? You were telling me yesterday that I should be going to college,' she says slowly.

I put my head in my hands – feeling utterly ashamed. What have I done? How could I not have known? I finally lift my head and say, 'But if I'd known I would have done things differently.'

'I tried but...none, well, none of you could see it or understand it,' she says, her words jumbling as though she's struggling to speak.

'You should have made me understand,' I say again, sighing in frustration.

She looks down at the cup in her hands before looking up at me and saying forcefully, 'You all change the subject…or if you do listen then you'll only listen so far. I can see it in your faces when you don't want to hear any more…you recoil from me, even though what I'm telling you is so tiny. You squirm in your seat and I see you look at the door as if you want to run through it, so I stop because I'm terrified of…' She breaks off and it's my turn to be unable to hold her gaze.

I take a deep breath, her words winding me and ripping at my gut.

'I don't want to lose the few friends I have left.'

'You're not going to lose your friends,' I dismiss.

'Really? So what happened to all the ones I had in school?' she demands.

'I never meant them,' I say shortly. 'I meant your real friends.'

'Yeah, well they saw something similar and I've not seen or heard from them in a year and a half, despite all their promises,' she tells me, her eyes not meeting mine before adding, so softly that it could be a whisper, 'I get that it's hard to listen to and see but…'

'…But you have to live it,' I say, guessing the ending of her sentence.

She simply nods.

'….I'm sorry,' I say regretfully. 'I just wish I'd known.'

Joyce sighs heavily, the weight of her woes deflating her lungs in exchange for a moment's relief. 'I didn't want you to look at me like you are now.'

'How? How am I looking at you?' I ask nervously, although I'm not sure I want to know.

'It doesn't matter,' she tells me.

'Joyce...' I begin but the words I was going to speak seem adrift.

'Even you're doing it now. Calling me Joyce: you've never called me that,' she remarks, her voice a false brightness.

'I never realised I was,' I say, running my hand through my hair and then flattening it all back down again because it feels odd being all up on end.

'I don't think they do either,' she tells me, taking a sip from her cup. 'They sometimes call me Joy and then they look shocked like I might tell them off or something.'

'Really?' I say, trying to push my smile back to its normal height.

'Yeah,' she says, trying to match my forced brightness. 'I'm sorry you had to spend the day here,' she adds.

'Are you kidding? This is the most peace and quiet I've had since I came home,' I say, sliding back into my jovial ways, and she looks relieved when I do, as though she was worried she had taken it from me. 'Are you ok, though?'

'I'm fine now...if you need to go—,' Joy says, her voice trailing away.

'No, no it's fine,' I say, unable to stop myself from glancing at the clock on the windowsill.

'I'm just going to spend the day in bed. I'm getting tired so I should probably...' Her voice trails away, her words lost into the unknown.

'You sure?' I ask, sitting forwards, reluctant to get up and leave her while at the same time being desperate to.

'It's fine, Logan,' she says briskly. I think she knows, I think she can tell that I'm desperate to get away from her and I feel terrible for it. I get up and move to open the front door with a haste out with my control, and I realise how much restraint has been keeping me here.

'Your jacket,' Joy says from behind me.

'Ah yeah,' I say, quickly grabbing it from the stairs and putting it back on. 'Call me if you need me to come back.'

It takes all I have not to run to the car. As I head out of her drive I glance in the mirror and see her standing in the doorway with her arms wrapped around herself. I consider turning around but I don't. I tell myself it's because I don't want to disturb her… but I know that's a lie.

I get out of view of her cottage before I pull the car off the road and stop in the turn into a field. I put my elbows on the steering wheel and rest my head in my hands. There have been few times in my life that I've felt as inadequate as I do now. Two years, two years and I was blind to it all. And I know she's been alone in this because if I know Joy, she won't speak to her aunt, sister or cousin about it. Had I really squirmed in my seat and looked to the nearest escape? I sigh a shuddering breath, the tension momentarily leaving my body before returning with a vengeance because I have a gut-wrenching feeling that I did. I tell myself it wasn't just me. She said that everyone did it, but that only makes it worse; it only makes her more alone and me more of a failure for not being the one who was better than the rest. All this time I credited myself for sticking by her when really she was the one sticking by me.

I sit back as I look out at the green fields and the hills around me. I shake my head in bitter frustration as I remember my Uncle Davey telling me yesterday to get her a seat and then later to take the jeep. He knew, he saw…so why couldn't I?….because I didn't want to, I realise shamefully. It was easier not to see, not to listen, and in doing so I isolated the person who needed enveloping. I made Joy protect me, shield me from her illness when I should have been protecting her.

Chapter Nine

The three do's and don'ts that I look for in a doctor.

Don't:

- Patronise me because I'm young. Youth does not equal stupidity.
- Speak to my aunt, the adult, rather than me…you know, the patient.
- Automatically presume that everything I say is a gross exaggeration and therefore dismiss it, because, after all, what do I know?

Do:

- Listen to me – You might learn something which will diagnose me.
- Talk to me – To further understand and diagnose me.
- Believe me – I'm not here because I love the decor of your waiting room.

'I see you've been diagnosed,' Dr Careless says brightly.

'No,' I say bluntly.

'It says here on your notes that you've been diagnosed with ME/CFS,' she says, looking at her computer screen.

'No,' I say again, glancing at my aunt.

'He said it was something that should be investigated,' my aunt explains.

'Well...I think that's what you have,' Dr Careless says brazenly. 'Here's a leaflet about a support group.'

She hands it to me like that's it, done and dusted, time to go. I've waited a month for this appointment and I've been in her office less than two minutes.

'Perhaps you could tell Joyce what ME *actually* is,' my aunt says pointedly.

'ME stands for myalgic encephalomyelitis or CFS which is chronic fatigue syndrome. We think it's caused by post-viral or bacterial infection which ties in with when you had glandular fever,' Dr Careless tells us.

'She never had glandular fever,' Aunt Beth says curtly.

'She had it when she was sixteen, that's when she first became unwell,' the doctor says with a false sweetness.

'The blood test for it was negative and she never even had a sore throat which is a pretty big symptom not to have,' Aunt Beth reminds her.

Dr Careless's lips pucker like she is sucking on something sour. 'Well, I think ME fits with her symptoms: the fatigue, joint and muscle pain, headaches...her difficulty sleeping.'

'What about Lyme disease?' my aunt asks. The name stirs something in my mind: I've heard that disease before but I don't know where.

'As we have discussed previously, the probability of her having Lyme disease is extremely low,' the doctor says, turning back to her computer and clicking away with the mouse. 'Yes, see, you have had three blood tests already for Lyme disease and they have all come back negative. It's not Lyme.'

'I'm still concerned it could be Lyme disease: the symptoms for Lyme and ME are very similar,' my aunt says. Her voice is steadfast but I can hear the edge of desperation creeping into it.

Dr Careless's lips are getting increasingly thin, her fingers dumbing off the edge of her seat. I can practically hear the words of "What do you know? I'm the one with the medical degree" going through her mind. After all, who are we, the great uneducated, to question her omnipotence?

'Do you live directly next to a forest?' she asks briskly, turning to me.

'No, we live next to fields,' I say meekly.

'Then you don't live in an area where you're at risk of getting Lyme,' she says sharply. 'And you told me previously that you've not had a bull's-eye rash, which you would have if you had Lyme disease.'

'What is cognitive behavioural therapy?' I ask, looking at the leaflet in my hand.

'It's a support group which will help you overcome the mental barriers which are stopping you from getting better,' Dr Careless says with the efficiency of a well-used party line.

I feel as though she's punched me. "Mental barriers" – is she saying I'm imagining this? That it's all in my mind?

'How long does it take to get better?' I ask quietly.

'A lot of people never get better,' Dr Careless says flippantly to her eighteen-year-old patient.

My aunt looks livid: she looks like she wants to pull the doctor by her neatly styled hair until she learns some tact.

'Is there any news about the second opinion we asked for?' my aunt says with forced politeness.

What little lips the doctor had visibly disappear. She looks like she's resisting the urge to glare as she turns to her computer and slaps each key until she finds what she wants. 'Your second opinion's been granted...it will be in Northcairn...with...ah, Dr Burk, he's a good friend of mine,' she says with a look of vindictive pleasure.

As my aunt and I leave Dr Careless's office we glance at each other with a sense of foreboding. We both know that at the first opportunity Dr Careless will phone Dr Burk and tell him all about me and my imaginary illness and my difficult aunt who refuses for me to be ignored and pushed aside by the medical profession.

***

'I think I'll make a list of your activities from before you were ill and what you're able to do now...and I'll make a list of all your symptoms, too,' my aunt says, more to herself than to me.

'Why?' I ask, not really caring about the answer. I sit back into the heavily cushioned chair of the coffee shop, trying to force myself to relax.

'I thought I could send it to the doctor before our appointment at Northcairn. I'll have to book a hotel for us once we get the date,' my aunt says before taking a deep sip from her steaming cup with apparent relish.

The coffee shop is quite busy today. I can't help but furtively watch all the people around us, talking, laughing, just enjoying their day. How can they carry on with life as though nothing's happened? So unaware and oblivious to the fact that mine's been taken away. I might never get better. I have ME but something inside me is telling me they're wrong. I have to disregard this notion; I have to because it's simply hope, toying and teasing me once more.

I envy these people, so relaxed and at ease. Of course I don't know them or their woes but they seem so light, so free, as though nothing burdens or concerns them. My aunt and I used to be one of you, I think to myself…but not anymore, not now.

'What made you think of Lyme disease?' I suddenly ask my aunt.

'You told me about it, remember?' she asks, studying me closely, her cup suspended between the table and her mouth. '… The man at Logan's farm told you about his wife: well, I presume it's his wife who has it? I did some research on it. I wish I had had time to do more but….' Her voice trails off.

I remember the man, Davey I think he's called, but I don't remember the conversation or the one in which I told my aunt.

'What is it?' I ask, taking my teaspoon and scooping a mouthful of fudge cake.

'You can get it from a tick bite,' she says.

'I don't remember being bitten,' I say, taking another bite of cake.

'You might not have noticed if you were bitten on your back or your feet or your scalp or…other hairy places,' she adds awkwardly.

'–Right,' I splutter, coughing on my piece of cake.

There's an uncomfortable silence before she adds with noticeable effort at normality, 'And they can be tiny, you know. I read they can be as small as a pinhead.'

'A pinhead?' I say sceptically.

Aunt Beth nods, her mouth full of cake. She puts her hand over her mouth. 'Mmh, yeah…I saw pictures online. The early symptoms are quite flu-like. You were bitten quite a few times as a child, but I never knew anything about Lyme disease.'

'I wasn't sick as a kid,' I say, finishing off my caramel latte.

'Well, I read that the disease can lie dormant in your body for years. I need to read more about it, but it's a possibility,' Aunt Beth says with a heavy sigh.

'Can we go?' I ask, noticing her empty cup which she keeps cradled in her hands, nurturing its fading warmth as the table next to us start laughing raucously.

We sit in silence most of the way home, allowing the radio to fill in the long gaps. My aunt takes the longer journey home, "the scenic route", the tourist people would call it. I'm glad that she does. I feel starved from the world, and the huge loch we drive alongside with the mountains behind it are so captivating that it nourishes me. Sometimes it feels as though the world starts and ends with the views from my windows, as though nothing can lie beyond them and I feel increasingly laden and suppressed as we glide over the roads which take us closer to the home that's both my cage and my castle.

My aunt drops me off at the cottage before heading to work. I go into the house and stand in the hall. It's quiet and still... I'm alone and shrunken, lost and unsure of what to do...I'm not imagining it, I'm not. I go upstairs and sit in my window seat, watching, mesmerised, as the clouds sink low onto the mountains, enveloping them into obscurity like this illness has done to me. I want to rest but I'm also restless, so I grab my laptop from my desk and hasten downstairs to the kitchen. I make myself a strong coffee as I wait for my laptop to turn on.

I type cognitive behavioural therapy (CBT) into the search box and click on the first website which comes up. I read that CBT is mainly used to treat anxiety and depression, but apparently it can be used to treat physical illness. Oh wait! Let me correct that – it cannot cure your physical issues, but it helps you to deal with them in a more positive way. I read about how it aspires to change your way of thinking, to see the positive amongst all the negatives which outweigh it. So you're sick and have lost your future, the majority of your friends and activities, and you're severely physically and mentally impaired but hey, at least you get to spend more time with the dog! It also gets you to look at the world differently, to appreciate the beauty and the good things around you. So basically what I subconsciously did earlier is what they think I need training to do. I don't doubt that it can help people, and when it does then all the better and in a way I'm envious because I don't think I'm one of them. I don't believe I'm passive – I don't sit thinking woe be me – but if I want to be upset every now and then, then I will be because as much as I have a duty to keep going, I also have the right to miss what I've lost.

I can feel my blood boiling as I change my search to Lyme disease. After thirty minutes I've not found much beyond lists of symptoms which could equally be ME and some information about ticks. I discover that they have an anaesthetic in their saliva so that you can't feel them biting and drawing blood from you. It's only when they stop feasting on your life-giving blood that you might feel something itchy on your leg or wherever the little sucker has bitten you. A tick's saliva also contains blood thinners to prevent the wound from clotting. I also discover that ticks can be found anywhere that there are animals, grass, woods or, well, just about everywhere.

I'm livid, absolutely livid because I could not be more at risk of getting a tick bite if I rolled in the heather naked! That moron with her arrogance in her title of Doctor was wrong on an epic scale. I live next to fields, with sheep, cows and wild deer in them. I worked on farms, I worked with animals, I walked up mountains through the heather and the bracken and I went cycling through the woods nearby – she knows all this. I know she knows all this because she even asked me when I entered her room if I had managed to get back to my hillwalking at all...It doesn't mean anything though, I remind myself. The symptoms are the same and the test for Lyme disease was negative. It's ME/CFS that I have. I tell myself it's natural to fight against a diagnosis that there may be no recovery from, but I can't help it. I turn off my laptop, it's done now, accept it, this may be all I get from life. I get to my feet with an unusual grace that's not belonged to me since before I was sick, fuelled by my anger, suppressed by my resignation. I fill the sink with water and clean the dishes, determined to do the few things I can get from this life.

Chapter Ten

The loch is as smooth as silk, a mirror to the hills and mountains behind it. Its peace and tranquility are perfected by the warmth of the sun upon my face as I sit on the bench near the loch. The walk to the bench is not far but even I'm startled by how much it took out of me. My aunt's standing by the loch's edge with Dog sitting smartly by her feet, excitement at the ball thrower in my aunt's hand making him wriggle where he sits. Aunt Beth throws the ball and the plastic thrower catapults it through the air, sending it far into the loch. Dog bounds into the water, his body sending ripples far and wide, distorting the perfection of the water's reflection, but that only makes me enjoy it more.

I've not been so good the past few weeks – it happens from time to time on this roller coaster of an illness, but its highs are too low and its lows are too steep, and each time I dip it takes even more for me to claw my way out of them.

I've gone off food and not for the first time. My aunt likes to claim that I'm not eating anything but that's untrue. I'm just not eating anything substantial, dry toast mostly. I just can't bring myself to eat anything – the look of it, the smell, texture and taste…I just….I can't. I did try forcing myself to eat. That's how I got through it the last time but I quickly stopped that tactic after a horrible few hours during which I had to battle to keep the contents of my stomach.

Since I've been ill I've found that I don't get hungry, not in the way I used to. I know when my body needs me to eat but I don't feel hunger. It's unusual for me to get cravings and when I do it tends to be for something bizarre which never lives up to the expectation I had for it. But I don't even feel my body's need for food just now. Some days the nausea is bad; sometimes there's just a pain in my stomach. Other days there's neither but I still can't eat. Even the idea of it makes my insides recoil.

After ten minutes my aunt comes over to me, much to the disappointment of Dog who's staring at the ground where his ball is, as though unable to understand why it's not moving of its own volition. Aunt Beth sits beside me and lifts her bag from under the bench, moving over slightly so that the bag can sit between us. From inside it she produces a flask and two plastic cups. After a moment she hands me a cup and I take a small sip. So far I've been fine with tea.

I take a deep breath of the fresh air. This is the only place I ever feel any sense of calm. It feels peaceful here, even with the chatter of the birds around us.

I tense as I see my aunt rummaging around her bag. I know what she's looking for and I know she'll find it, but I still hope that she doesn't.

'Do you want a biscuit?' she asks casually enough…but I can hear the desperation in her voice.

She holds the plastic container out for me and I look at the selection of biscuits inside it. She must have opened every packet in the cupboards to get such a variety. She hates doing that. We always got into trouble as children when we opened another packet without finishing the one that was open. I shift uncomfortably on the bench as my guilt over the worry I'm causing her rises up through my gut. I hesitantly take the plainest biscuit in the box and take a reluctant bite. It feels foreign in my mouth and I want to spit it out, but I don't. I swallow my mouthful and trace its displeasing journey down into my stomach where it sits disproportionately heavy and uncomfortable...but the joyous relief on my aunt's face nearly makes it worthwhile.

'Here, do you want another one? It's the last one of that kind in the box,' she says hopefully, holding out another biscuit of the same kind, her body tensed like I'm a bird that might take flight at any movement. I wish I hadn't taken the first one now – she thinks I like these ones; she thinks she's struck gold in finding something that I can eat. I take it and Aunt Beth's entire body relaxes. I'll take what pain comes after if it means I can take away hers.

***

I go for a nap as soon as we get home. It's something I've taken to doing in the afternoons. I don't actually fall asleep, I just kind of doze, but it can be surprisingly restorative at times. I think I've been lying here for an hour or two when my aunt comes into my dining room and I can tell by her movements that something has happened.

'What is it?' I ask, propping myself up on my elbow.

'I know what's wrong with you,' she says feverishly, sitting on the edge of my bed. 'It's Lyme disease, I'm sure of it, all your symptoms fit.'

'They fit ME, too, I looked it up,' I say, letting myself collapse back onto the sofa bed.

'I know, so did I, but then I put in the specific symptoms

you have alongside Lyme disease and I got heaps of information. I put in every symptom of yours that I could think of and they all matched with Lyme but they don't with ME,' she tells me, brushing her brown hair behind her ear impatiently.

'But I was tested for Lyme,' I remind her, watching her darkened form against the light from the hall.

'The hospital's tests aren't accurate. I've been reading news articles and blogs about people who've had more than ten blood tests before they got a positive one. Their stories are so similar to yours that it could be you they're talking about.'

'Right,' I say solemnly, unable to match her enthusiasm. She seems to think this is a great breakthrough, but I don't see how it changes anything.

'I'm going to write that letter now we have a date for your second opinion,' she says, getting up from the bed and leaving my room with a newfound vigour.

And that's exactly what she does over the next week. Each evening she sits with her laptop and writes her increasingly long letter. She deletes entire sections and rewrites them. At one point she deletes the entire thing, saying that it's too emotional and that she needs it to sound more medical so that they will take it more seriously. She gives me the laptop at times so that I can add any symptoms she's missed. It saddens me that we even have to do this, that the people who have sworn an oath and who are paid generously to care, simply don't. I'm not naïve: most doctors didn't become doctors simply for the joy of treating patients. For a lot of doctors the patients are the worst part of the job. They put themselves through all those years of training because they love the medicine, but the pressure they're put under stifles that fascination away so that solving an enigma like me becomes laborious.

After over a week the letter's done. It's sitting on the kitchen table when I get up that morning. I try to ignore it as I make my breakfast but it keeps catching my eye. Once I've eaten I can't put off my aunt's instructions to read it any longer.

Dear Dr Burk,

Thank you for your appointment.... I can feel my concentration ebbing already so I skip the niceties.

Joyce's activities before she became ill.

Joyce has always been very active. Living in a rural farming community she has spent the majority of her life outside. From childhood onwards, Joyce has participated in a number of outdoor activities, including cross-country running and cycling races, hillwalking, tennis, swimming, and was in training for Munro-bagging at the time she became unwell. She was in full-time education and worked full-time in the school holidays at a local coffee shop and had several interviews for university, all of which she had to cancel due to her deteriorating health.

Joyce now.

Joyce's abilities are extremely limited. Having been forced to leave school early and being unable to work or socialise have resulted in Joyce becoming extremely isolated. Her daily activities are greatly restricted due to her health and she is not able to leave the house unaccompanied. She can't do any of the hobbies or activities she once enjoyed so much. Joyce has currently lost two years of her life due to this illness.

The letter then goes on about blood tests and why my aunt believes "very strongly" that it is Lyme disease I have and why the diagnosis of ME/CFS is incorrect and how the evidence proves this. What shocks and interests me the most is my list of symptoms: there are over thirty and I know there will be ones we've forgotten:

- *Excessive thirst.*
- *Burning and tightness in throat due to thirst.*
- *Disturbed sleep – unable to get to sleep, difficulty in staying asleep and feeling unrested when waking.*
- *Mental exhaustion.*
- *Physical fatigue.*
- *Mobility severely impaired – on good day can walk short distance, on bad day needs help to walk, e.g. use of stick and furniture to get about.*
- *Balance badly impaired – can lose balance when standing still and walking.*
- *Poor appetite, nausea, weight loss.*
- *Hot flushes and at times feverish.*
- *Feeling cold – hands and feet can turn blue.*
- *Bad days – needs help with daily living, e.g. eating, getting to the bathroom.*
- *Intolerance to heat and cold.*
- *Sensitivity to light and touch.*
- *Sensitivity to sound – ringing in the ears.*
- *Irritable – anxious – difficulty in being in unfamiliar places or with unknown people.*
- *Headaches – migraine?*
- *Joint pain, stiff neck and shoulders.*
- *Joints can frequently be heard cracking.*
- *Muscle pain.*
- *Bone pain.*
- *Pain in the bottom of the feet.*
- *Heart racing – pulse fast even when sitting resting.*
- *Heart palpitations.*
- *Poor concentration.*

- *Memory impairment.*
- *Difficulty speaking – loses bits of conversation, can't find words to express what she wants to say.*
- *Pins and needles, numbness.*
- *Twitching – often in the face and right side of body but can be anywhere.*
- *Rippling – muscles move independently.*
- *Weakness.*
- *Rashes – often on chest and back and sometimes hands. Looks like lots of pin marks.*
- *Feeling of heaviness.*
- *Occasionally collapsing.*
- *Difficulty thinking – brain fog.*

The letter then goes on about what areas my aunt has researched: lupus, MS, sarcoidosis, ME/CFS, fibromyalgia: it just goes on and on.

It's so huge, this thing that's wrong with me. I don't normally let myself think about it – it's too dangerous a thing to do because now I feel winded, beaten and broken to my core. How can a person have all those symptoms?...but I do and I can experience them all within one day. It's no wonder I'm so exhausted. It reaffirms to me that it's not in my head. I'd never seen or heard of some of those symptoms before I became ill, so how could I have made them up?.....but what if I did? What if I saw them on TV and forgot? After all, how can one person have so many symptoms?

I stand up. I feel feeble and unstable as I head down the hall towards my room but I pause, my mind working at the doubts within it. I force myself to walk faster – my heart pounding with fear, and it works. I can move faster than my body was telling me I could. I'm passing the cabinet when I lose my balance and my leg gives out from under me, sending me crashing painfully into the cabinet, my ribs colliding into the wooden edge as I knock a large china bowl onto the floor. I slump to the floor as broken as the shattered pieces of bowl around me, my ribs aching with what I'm sure will develop into bruising. I'm not sure what that proved: that it's all in my head or that my body was slowing me down so that I could get to where I needed to be without injury. It's like some of the times when I go out of the house, my body slows, and then when I get home it releases what reserves it was holding back, allowing me to move more freely because it seems to know I'm home. It seems to know there's nothing unexpected to come; it knows where each step will take me...and what about the times when I'm so ill I can barely move at all, when all the willpower in the world can't hasten my steps.

Chapter Eleven

The five most awkward questions for the chronically ill to answer:

- 'Sooo - what have you been up to?'....Ehhh nothing, oh yeah and a bit more of nothing.

- 'Do they know how long it will take for you to get better?'....Well, if they haven't figured out what's wrong with me yet, then I doubt they have a timetable for my recovery.

- 'You hurt your leg?' the complete stranger asks, looking at my walking stick...There are two types of people who ask this. There are the nosy people to whom I feel I should give the answer – Oh, I have a massive injury. I was bitten by my vicious pet hamster. And then there are those genuinely nice people who are interested in your well-being, even if they don't know you, to whom I give the truth.

- 'Are you contagious?' they ask as they freeze with their arms outstretched, about to hug me....Ehhh...Huh, I'm not entirely sure but my aunt and Dog have been sharing my air and they're not sick, so I'm guessing your thirty-minute visit will be safe enough.

- 'What do you do all day? You must get so bored being at home all the time?'....Firstly, as we've already established,

I don't do anything. Secondly, in order to be bored one must have the energy to do something, which I don't. I would be truly delighted and honoured for the burden of boredom to descend upon me.

My aunt and I are going to Northcairn for four days. We leave tomorrow: the second day I will rest, the third day is my appointment, and on the fourth day we come back. I told my aunt I would be fine coming home the day after the appointment. I hope it's true because in truth I just said that because I was worried about how much it was costing her for another night. My little sister Sarah's coming to look after Dog while we're away. My Aunt Beth's picking Sarah up from the train station on her way home from work. They should be here soon. I sigh heavily, the anxiety chewing away at my intestines at the prospect and knowledge that we're leaving tomorrow for the appointment. This doctor we're meeting is our last chance. After this there's nowhere left to go within the system and Aunt Beth is placing all of her hope in his healing hands.

I keep glancing at my phone as I put things into my bag for going to Northcairn. I'm not surprised I haven't heard from Logan since the day I was taken unwell in front of him. I did get a message from him later that day, asking how I was, but beyond that I've not heard a thing. And I'm not expecting a reply to the message I sent about my second opinion but it would be nice if I got one; it would be nice to know I could still count him as a friend, but after what he saw…I'm not sure I can. I wonder if Logan will become like the other few who keep in touch by message and never in person; our conversations instigated by me and never them, I often wonder why I continue to keep in touch with these people who I once called friends. The better and lighter part of me sympathises. It says I understand how hard it must be for them; it tells me not to get annoyed when they avoid and ignore my offers to meet up; it tells me not to be disheartened by my pitiful and near beseeching offers to cater to whatever time or date they need, just in the hope of seeing them. It reminds me to be grateful that they do *always* reply. But the darkest and deepest part of me pities their weakness the way I'm sure they pity mine. It resents their cowardice; it despises the ease with which they get to live their lives.

My phone beeps on the bed beside my bag and I hate how I hasten to grab it, but it's only Amy. She's home this weekend and wanted to meet up, but my aunt and I are going to Northcairn. We've been messaging for the past hour and a half about the triangle she managed to get herself into with two boys. I'm trying to be a good friend by being there for her, but if the choice between two kind, handsome and funny guys is really the biggest worry she has in her life – then I truly give up. Her woes are insignificant to me, but still I reply to each message she sends, going over the same points we went over thirty minutes ago. I force my frustration back, though. I know how lucky I am to have what few friends I have left, and dismissing their problems won't encourage them to stick around. Telling her to get a grip and pick one is a poor repayment for the visits she bestows upon me. Our relationships have become one of mutual difficulty, each struggling to be around the other who once complemented them. Our contrasts now differ so greatly from each other that neither side knows how to be around the other; my problems are too huge, my life too small, whereas their lives are too huge, their problems too small. Yet still we do this dance of mutual duty.

Why they do it instead of leaving like the rest is unknown to me. It's a question that I can't fathom an answer to, and if I'm honest I'm not sure it's a question I want answered because it's harder to leave someone inside a sinking ship when everyone else has already left. In a way I'm glad Amy has come to me with her problem, it feels like a hint of normality, and everyone always came to Joy with their worries and dilemmas but no one ever comes to Joyce. I'm not used to people wanting my opinion anymore and it feels nice to have her need me as much as I need her.

I'm zipping up my bag as my aunt's car pulls into the drive. I watch the car come to a halt as I wrap my arms around myself, the knots in my stomach pulling tight. I unzip my bag with a sudden desire to reaffirm what I've packed; I know I'm just buying time, putting off the moment I have to see Aunt Beth and Sarah. I don't know why I feel so anxious; I know it's foolish but I don't know how to make it stop. I listen for them coming in through the back entrance, the thump as bags are dropped onto the stone floor and as voices fill the kitchen and infiltrate the hall. I glance at my guard: his head is unmoving from his paws as he looks up at me as though he knows, unlike me, that there's no threat to be had. I freeze like a mouse playing dead at the sound of someone coming down the hall, hoping for its prey to pass them by, but the footsteps stop outside my door. I know it's Sarah by the sound of her tread. I clutch at the mound of socks I've been taking out of my bag and stacking against my chest as she knocks on the door and opens it. Realising how ridiculous I must look with my socks clutched to my chest, I hasten to drop them into the bag.

'Hi.....' Sarah says putting her head around the door, extending the word so that it sounds five times longer than it actually is. 'What are you doing?' she adds, giving me a funny look.

'Packing,' I say awkwardly.

She comes into my dining room and extends her arms. Her wavy, auburn hair, more brown than mine, falls across her shoulders as she leans in to wrap me in a huge hug. I hug her back, her delicately sweet perfume both pleasing and assaulting my nostrils. I'm uncomfortably aware of her fingers around my ribs.

Sarah looks me over as we part, but she doesn't say anything about my thinned frame. I've actually put weight on since I've clawed my way out of my dip, but I'm still quite a bit thinner than the last time she saw me. She's as impeccably dressed as always, her clothes smart but casual, comfy but fitted, stylish but practical. The style might not be completely mine, but the essence is so similar that I feel as though I'm looking at a mirror image of who I once was.

'You look nice,' I say, trying to sound bright, but the sadness creeps in nonetheless.

'Thanks,' she says brightly, oblivious to any other tone which is not complimentary. She sprawls herself across my sofa bed but then sits up, staring into my bag. 'What's with all the socks?'

'I was checking I had enough,' I say, running my hand through my hair nervously.

Sarah looks at me pityingly. I pretend to check my phone for messages that aren't there just so I don't have to look at her. Sarah reaches into my bag and takes my socks out, leaving five behind.

'I only need four,' I say meekly.

'You'd packed about twenty,' Sarah says, grossly exaggerating. 'It's spare…in case you stand in a puddle and your shoes aren't waterproof.'

'Right,' I say, trying to make my smile match hers; she laughs so I think I succeeded.

'GIRLS!' my aunt shouts. 'DINNER!'

As we enter the kitchen my aunt gestures for us to serve. She has the phone pressed to her ear and is saying something about a circuit-breaker to whoever is on the other end of the line as she slips out of the room. Sarah helps me plate up the beef pie, potatoes and vegetables in time for my Aunt Beth's return. The three of us sit at the table, a break from usual custom. Aunt Beth and Sarah seem to have an endless supply of things to talk about and I listen quietly as my aunt tells Sarah all about the new office buildings she's been working in at Brewers Road in the town. Her words are spilling out of her in an almost feverish fashion, as though she's been storing it all up, waiting for the moment when someone would ask...even though I ask. Granted, I'm not as eager an audience as Sarah, but still I ask. I thought our lack of news was mutual but evidently not. The soft lines around Aunt Beth's eyes crinkle into a smile at Sarah's enthusiastic remarks. I pick at my meal as Sarah takes her turn to tell us her news. I sit mostly in silence, telling myself it's nice to hear about the things Sarah's been up to, and that doesn't hurt to hear her do the things I can no longer do.

My Aunt Beth and Sarah have barely finished their last mouthfuls when I stand up and begin to clear away the plates. They offer to help but I don't take them up on their offer. I'm glad for any excuse to leave the table, even if it is just to the sink and back. I linger by the sink for as long as I can, scraping flakes of pastry and gravy into the bin underneath it. It's easier over here, away from the weight of performance which hangs about me at the table. It's hard to pay attention, to smile at the appropriate moment and laugh in the correct places when there's more than one person before me. I watch them speak, struggling to be a part of the conversation, the art of which seems so effortless to the other two. My brain lags behind, their words interchanging too rapidly for my mind to understand and comprehend. At times I want to say things, but by the time my mind catches up and thinks of a reply the conversation's moved on. The point I was going to make becomes irrelevant or they don't understand what I mean when it's no longer in reference to what they're now talking about. It's as if I'm watching live TV but listening to the conversation in slow motion. I always end up sitting back against my chair, feeling divided from them by the expanse of my shrinking mind. The unwitting looks they give and remarks of "What do you mean?" when I fail to make sense are sharply degrading because I don't know what I mean – I've already forgotten the thought leading up to my words.

Come nine o'clock I make my excuses and say my goodnights before heading to bed, with Dog sneaking as stealthily as my rising anxiety into bed with me.

After a long while I get up and head through to the bathroom. On the way back to my room, I pause in the hall at the sound of my aunt's and sister's voices. They moved a couple of hours ago to the comfort of the sitting room, their hushed voices creeping past my dining room before the door of the sitting room shut behind them. I can't make out what they're saying but they sound so happy that it makes me smile, while at the same time it fills me with sadness. I ease myself down onto the bottom step of the stairs, nostalgic to hear more. It's been so long since I've heard my aunt laugh like that; she never laughs like that with me. I can almost picture them in the sitting room together, steaming cups in hand, the warm fire comforting in the flickering of its majestic flames. I wrap my arms around myself, shiver in the cold air of the darkened hall. I want to join them, to be a part of whatever joke or story they've shared. I want to laugh as they are now, for the noise to fill the room so completely that it must escape through every crevice of space into the rooms around it. I want to be Joy – Joy was both creator of and participant in such a simple and glorious thing as laughter, but Joy's not here and I don't know how to get her back.

I cling onto the banister, whether to help me up or hold me down I'm not sure. I remember my friend hesitating to hug me, the look of horror as she realised what she was doing, the shock on her face as she asked me if I was contagious as though she had never meant to ask it out loud. I realise now that it's not my illness that's contagious…it's my misery. It seeps from me into anyone nearby me and I realise now, listening to my aunt's light laughter, just how great her exposure has been. I know what will happen if I go into the sitting room: my aunt and sister will fall silent; what conversation and laughter ensue will be stifled, even if I pretend and laugh along, too.

I rise heavily to my feet, my fingers and toes aching with the chill which is leaching into my bones. I go to my room and slowly shut the door, stifling their happy tones as their voices erupt into laughter more harmonic and jarring than any symphony. I lie in the darkness, wonder if their laughter will remain, if it will come so easily after my appointment in a couple of days. I hope I'm wrong, I hope my aunt's hopes are not wasted.

Chapter Twelve

Despite all my organising the previous day, I still felt rushed as we packed the car and prepared to leave for Northcairn, and although there was no time we had to leave by, I still hastened to gather my things and myself as though there was a strike and unmovable deadline.

Aunt Beth's waiting for me in the car as I go to the bathroom for what must be the fifth time this afternoon. I say goodbye to Dog and Sarah one last time before getting into the car and fastening my belt with the same sense of foreboding as someone going to the noose. I put on my sunglasses to shade my eyes from the bright afternoon sun as my aunt starts the engine and drives slowly down the drive. I watch in the side mirror as Sarah and my fortress house disappear from sight. It seems bizarre to me that I won't be sleeping within the stone walls of the cottage for the next three nights – it's been two, maybe three years since I've slept anywhere else.

It will take five hours to get to the city of Northcairn. As we drive along less familiar roads, I wonder how many days and weeks it would have taken those before me, with their trudging steps and horses' hooves. After an hour and a half, I decide that five hours in the car is trial enough. The vibrations of the engine make my neck stiffen into an aching mass; my hips, too, feel like a mass of hard material which resists and fights painfully against every jolt or movement of the car.

We stop part way at one of the larger shops and my aunt goes in to get us something to eat. I stretch my neck and shoulders as best as I can while I wait. I even stand outside of the car for a few minutes but the car fumes, movement and noises of the cars and people with their trolleys make me edgy. I'd like to stretch my legs, maybe walk around the car a couple of times, but I can't bring myself to let go of the door handle. When I do finally make myself let go of the handle, I only moved as far as the bonnet before another car suddenly swings into the empty space in front of me, startling me to my core. My heart pounding, I hasten with stumbling legs back into the car, hating how vulnerable and exposed I feel against the world and its fast-moving occupants whose speed and frequent impatience towards me feel like a physical threat as sure and as dangerous as any knife held to my throat.

When my aunt returns we have a picnic of bread, mini-sausages and crisps before we set off again.

'Do you need to stop?' my aunt asks, glancing over at me as I try and stretch my legs. 'Did you not get out and have a walk around when we stopped?'

I ignore her question and instead take my phone from my bag under the pretence of messaging Amy, but truthfully I'm checking for any messages from Logan. It's the not knowing that irritates me. If I knew the answer I could forget about it. I want to ask him if we're still friends, but I'm not sure if that's really the right thing to do. It's what used to irritate me the most, the way my estranged friends hung around the fringes of my life, trying to leave but never quite having the courage to do so. I would have preferred they were straight with me, brutally blunt. Instead, when the ground beneath my feet was taken, I was left with stepping stones of friends that I couldn't rely on, unsure of which would crumble and which were steadfast.

'Aunt Beth...?' My voice starts out quiet and trails away in a whisper.

I look out of the window at the roughed hillside we're driving through. Large rock formations stick out from the ground, some jutting up high while others remain embedded at ground level, where the thick heather and coarse grass can't grow upon them. Every now and then we drive past a waterfall which cascades over the rocks, its tracks traceable across and down the hillside like veins in the ground.

'Yes?' my aunt asks gently.

I continue looking out of the window; I had hoped she hadn't heard me. The sky's clouded over now but still I wear my sunglasses. I tried taking them off but it was still too bright without them.

'Why...why don't people like being around sick people?' I ask, turning to look at her. My question is so simply put that it makes me feel childish.

I watch my aunt's chest rise with the deep breath she's silently taken.

'I think sickness reminds people how frail they are and how quickly things can change. I mean, if someone as active and healthy as you can become so....' Aunt Beth's voice hangs in the air as though searching for the right word. Crippled, I want to supply for her. Personally, I think it's rather accurate, but of course my aunt thinks otherwise. Her words are softer, more gentle than mine. '...Unwell, then so can they.'

'What else?' I ask, her answer not satisfying my question.

'I think illness reminds people of death and, although a lot of people won't admit it, I think the majority of people are scared of dying,' she says, her eyes glancing to the mirror at the car behind us and back to the road again.

'Are you afraid of dying?' I ask as the car behind overtakes us at an alarming speed.

Aunt Beth hesitates, her hands moving to the top of the steering wheel. I can practically hear the debate going on inside her head: tell the truth or avoid the question.

'Yes, I'm afraid of dying,' she tells me, her hands sliding back to their original position at either side of the wheel. 'Are you?'

'No,' I say truthfully, looking back out of the window. The sun is shining through cracks in the thick clouds, holding clumps of heather and rock within its pools of light.

No, I'm not afraid of death, I'm afraid of living like this forever. That hooded figure in a black cloak is not the enemy to me as it is to others. We share something, this figure and I. We share the knowledge that death is a mercy against fates far worse. For those of you who fear or simply don't like death's presence, I congratulate you because, whether you realise it or not, you have found something worth living for.

***

It takes a total of five and a half hours to get to Northcairn, twenty of which were spent trying to find the hotel. When we arrive my aunt leaves me in the car so that she can check in and find our room before coming back out for me. My aunt helps me ease my stiff frame out of the car, my hips feeling like rusted hinges reluctant to straighten from their bent position. I get my bag from the back seat while Aunt Beth gets her things from the boot. Once Aunt Beth shuts the boot and shuffles all her bags onto one arm, she holds out her other arm for me to link with hers, a tired smile upon her face. I take her arm, relieved to have something for my aching and unbalanced limbs to hold onto while at the same time trying not to remember the man at Logan's farm offering me his. The hotel corridor is long and windowless, but I'm glad for the walk which eases the stiffness from my limbs.

Our en suite room has two single beds, a table and chair, a couch, wardrobe and a TV mounted on the wall. It's cheap (for Northcairn) and not entirely cheerful but it's clean and that's all my aunt and I care about. We pick at some of the food from our picnic before getting ready for bed. When I come out of the bathroom I wait for my aunt to go in before getting changed into my nightclothes. I hesitate before climbing into the crisp, white sheets, feeling dirty in my faded pyjamas which have long since lost their shape. I slip under the tightly pulled-up sheets, comforted by the cocooned feeling I have beneath them.

When I wake the following morning, I feel as though someone's smashed a shovel over my head and then proceeded to run me over with a bus. I wish I was exaggerating but I'm not. When I look over at my aunt I see she's sitting up in bed, with a cup in one hand and a book in the other, the light above her head shining down upon her like an artificial ray of sunshine. When she sees I'm awake she gets up from her bed and moves to get the kettle. I close my eyes and listen to her move to the bathroom where she fills the kettle from the sink. You need to get up, my brain says strongly, but another voice sneaks into my mind. I picture it as the voice of my body which whispers soothingly,

Just a minute longer. My aunt returns and slowly the rumble from the kettle fills the room. Open your eyes, my brain orders as the kettle clicks off the boil and the water is poured into the cup. *No,* the other voice says sulkily. She's about to come over, you need to open your eyes. *Why? Why are you asking me to do something that hurts?* You're ill, everything hurts, now get up! I hear the small thump of the tea bag being dropped into the bin. With my eyes barely open, my aunt comes over and helps me sit up with the aid of the extra cushions from inside the wardrobe before handing me my tea.

'Thanks.' My muttered and slurred words feel inadequate to express my gratitude for this reviving sustenance.

I bring the cup towards my lips but even before I've taken a sip I can feel the scalding heat coming off of it. *You could have been sleeping while that cooled, you know.* Oh shut up, my mind snarls.

Once I'm more awake and alert, Aunt Beth tells me she's going out to get us something for dinner. She leaves me a chocolate pastry for breakfast and the last of our picnic food from last night. She brushes my hair back tenderly with her hand before heading out of our room with the remark that tomorrow will be a big day.

In a way I'm glad she's gone out: it means I can rest in a way that I can't when she's here, but as soon as she leaves I feel on edge. The habitual fear of something happening is a sharp thorn in my side. Irrational though I know it is, my mind runs through all the horrible things that could happen: a mugging, a hit-and-run, a heart attack, kidnapping. It's an endless stream of possibilities to haunt my untamable mind until she returns safe and sound.

Chapter Thirteen

Question: What is the most important and powerful thing you can say to someone with a chronic/unknown illness?

Answer: I BELIEVE YOU.

Bonus points: To say it with complete understanding and honesty.

The walls of the hospital waiting room are a lurid shade of orange, which reminds me of children's crayons. Vacant chairs line the walls except in the corners, where small tables with out-of-date magazines have been placed, their corners curling and bent under all the hands that have held them. From her seat beside me, Aunt Beth's studying the bulletin board to the right of us. Leaflets for breastfeeding mothers, mobility chairs, cancer and drink and alcohol support groups fight for attention on the overcrowded board. But my attention is fixed upon the row of chairs in front of us, where strange oval marks have been left on the wall. It takes me a while to realise that the marks are from people resting their heads on the wall. I look around the room at the unpleasantly grimy and discoloured marks, evidence, if ever it was needed, of the great unwashed, a membership I resent holding a pass to.

My appointment's meant to be at half-four but it's nearing

five o'clock. Despite the uncomfortableness and my growing tiredness, I don't mind waiting. I was glad to have received a later appointment – it meant I didn't have to rush when I woke up this morning/afternoon.

'Joyce Jack?' asks a middle-aged nurse in a dark uniform, appearing in the doorway.

I smile nervously and get to my feet. My aunt does the same and we both walk towards the nurse who immediately takes off down the corridor. She's halfway down it by the time I get to the threshold of the waiting room. I hasten my steps in a pathetic attempt to keep up. The nurse pauses at the end of the corridor and although she shows no outward signs of impatience I still feel a pushing pressure at my back to hurry up. Why do they always do that? Why can't they walk alongside me like my aunt? There's no need to show off your mature, healthy legs; my young, old ones already know their inferiority. I grab onto the railing that runs along the wall as I wobble unsteadily, my weak legs unable to deliver the balance I need for the speed I'm asking of them. It's a hurtful reminder of how slow I've become. It's easy when you live alone to fool yourself with the idea that what you feel is what everyone feels – your slow pace is the same frustrating crawl as the rest of the world's – your aches and pains no worse than anyone else's, but then an occasion occurs in which your illusion is pierced by the world outside. Whether something infiltrates your caged castle or you're forced to break it yourself by leaving the house, the painful shattering outcome of disillusionment is the same.

When we reach the nurse, she shows us into a room full of cupboards and worktops. She takes my weight, height and pulse before leading us to the doctor's room. The nurse knocks on the door, then waits for a moment before opening and holding the door for us to walk through before shutting it loudly behind us.

'Joyce?' Doctor Burk asks, looking at me but without getting up from his seat.

'Yes,' I say meekly, hoping to seem friendly by giving a small smile.

He returns my gesture and invites us to take a seat in the two chairs by the side of his desk. His friendly features have a calming effect and I slowly release the breath I was holding, the tension in my muscles too guarded to be eased, but my breathing does slow.

'And you must be Mum?' he asks my aunt. His face is shaven clean, his black hair is heavy streaked with grey, his shirt and trousers neatly ironed.

'I'm Joyce's aunt,' my aunt says, putting her handbag on the ground by her feet.

'Is your mother not able to come?' Doctor Burk asks.

'I live with my aunt,' I explain.

'Ahh, I see,' Doctor Burk says, turning in his chair and opening the file in front of him as though its paper shield can protect him from the awkwardness that's settled between the three of us. 'I understand that you're here for a second opinion?'

He looks at me expectantly but I'm not sure what he wants me to say so I simply nod.

'I've read over your file and you've had an extensive investigation into your health. I'm not sure what more I can add,' he says, closing over the file.

I'm beginning to feel like this is some sick and twisted game of pass the parcel. Each doctor feeling the parcel just long enough to be able to throw their hands up and say, 'I've no idea what's inside,' while hastily chucking it to the next doctor before the music can stop.

'Did you get my letter?' my aunt puts in.

'I did,' he says reservedly, leaning back in his chair.

'Then you'll know I'm concerned about Lyme disease,' Aunt Beth says.

'Yes, I can understand why you *might* be concerned...' he says slowly, as though choosing his words carefully, '...but Joyce has had several tests for Lyme disease and all of them have been negative. From your notes you've said you've not had a bull's-eye rash, and not all of her symptoms fit Lyme disease.'

'But the testing isn't accurate, is it? And some scientists believe that up to 90% of people with Lyme don't get a bull's-eye rash,' my aunt says, her voice growing in confidence.

'There is a certain amount of discrepancy in the tests, which is probably why your doctors back home have done so many Lyme tests. I haven't read that report that you've read so I'm afraid I can't give an opinion on it.'

'Which blood tests have been used?' my aunt asks. I can hear it in her voice, her gearing up to use her trump card, her line of questioning luring him into her trap.

'Let me just check,' he says, flipping through the file on his desk. You would think, seeing as it has my name on it, that I'd be allowed a look. I did ask one of my doctors once but the answer was a firm no. 'Both Western blot and ELISA tests have been done.'

'Right,' my aunt says, her voice depleted. I look over at her to see that she's looking into the corner of the room; she looks shrunken like a balloon that's had half the air let out of it.

Why isn't she saying anything? Or doing anything? What's happened to all the research she's done to argue her case?

'What about all the symptoms that don't match ME and CFS?' I say.

'What symptoms?' Doctor Burk asks flippantly.

I wrack my blank mind, begging it to give me one. 'The twitching and rippling.'

'Twitching can be caused by dehydration … anxiety which I believe is one of your symptoms; also you may have a vitamin B deficiency if you're struggling to eat properly,' he states.

'What about the fatigue? About being so weak I can barely walk at times,' I say desperately.

He looks down at his hands, I don't know why but I think he's ashamed and I don't think it's because of me.

'Unfortunately,' he says, looking up at me again, 'that is a common part of ME/CFS. Have you been to any support groups?'

'No, there's only one in our area and it's during the week. I've no way of getting to it,' I tell him.

'It's on the third floor,' my aunt suddenly puts in.

'I'm sorry?' Doctor Burk says. So you should be, I think to myself.

'The support group. They hold it on the third floor of a building that has no lift and it's on at nine in the morning. Do you know how ill she would be if I woke her at that time and then asked her to climb three flights of stairs when she can barely manage one?'

I watch the doctor, determined not to look at my aunt. I never knew she had considered taking me to CBT (cognitive behavioural therapy) or that she had gone so far as to find out the time and even checked out the building it was held in.

'Well…I think it would be beneficial for you to go. I know

there are a lot of psychological elements to ME/CFS–'

'Are you saying this is all in my head?' I demand, cutting him off. I'm sick of doctors telling me I'm imagining it all without actually saying it, and for the first time in two years my brain is suddenly working at a speed in which I can at least attempt to hold them to the hidden meaning of their words.

'Yes,' he says brutally but honestly.

I glare at the hinges on the doctor's door. I wish I could say I was angry, shocked, hurt, sad or ever scared but I don't feel anything.

***

Back in our hotel room, I watch my aunt go through the routine of making us a cup of tea: cups, tea bags, milk, hot water, stir, squeeze, dump, done, the ritual's so ingrained that it brings comfort in chaos, purpose in the meaninglessness. Aunt Beth hands me a cup and then sits on her bed, looking lost now she has nothing to do but wait for her tea to cool enough for her to drink it. I reach for the remote on the table by my bed and turn on the TV, its noise, movement and colour synthetically filling the void where hope used to be. After a while my aunt gets up and collects the remainder of the food she bought yesterday and brings it to my bed.

'I'm not hungry,' I say quietly.

'You have to eat,' my aunt says despondently.

As though to set an example, she makes herself a crisp sandwich and sits on her bed to eat it. My instinct is to rebel against her, to watch her eat without eating anything myself. I'm not hungry; I don't want to eat, so why should I? But nonetheless

I take a breakfast bar from the selection and begin to eat it. I think enough discord has been endured for one day.

My aunt only eats half her sandwich before she gives up and puts it in the bin.

'I'm going for a shower,' she tells me dispassionately, gathering her things as though she's in a hurry.

'I'm sorry,' I say, my voice a mere whisper as she opens the door of the bathroom and disappears through it. I don't think she heard me, not over the sound of the TV she was standing opposite to as she entered the bathroom. Maybe it's a good thing she never heard, but nonetheless I say it again to the empty room, 'I'm so sorry.'

Now my aunt's out of the room I turn the volume on the TV down to a level that doesn't hurt my ears, but the sound of car engines and horns soon overtakes what quiet the reduced volume gave, reminding me how far from home we are. I bring my knees up to my chest and wrap my arms around them as a chill spreads through my body, seeping like fast-spreading damp through my bones and into my marrow. I hear the water from the shower hitting the base of the bath like heavy rain bouncing off the pavement and after a moment I hear something else, a muffled sound not congruent with someone taking a shower. I slide off my bed which is beside the wall of the bathroom and press my ear against the cool wall, listening hard. The sound of my aunt's ragged breathing confirms what I already know, that she's crying and she's doing so alone.

I sink down onto the floor and press myself against the wall, my ear pushed so hard against the cream wall that it hurts. I hear her sniff over the sound of the shower and sigh heavily as though she's trying to expel all the sorrow inside of her. I wish I could be with her, comfort her and make everything right. I press my hand against the wall, my body pushed tight against it as though my proximity will somehow comfort her, as though I might absorb her pain through the wall which divides us, the way my body absorbs the coolness from the plaster. I imagine her sitting on the closed lid of the toilet, the steam from the shower swirling around her and filling the room like mist on the mountains back home. I know that the bathroom door is locked, and even if it wasn't, she wouldn't want me to enter. If it was me in there my aunt would barge the door down, refusing to allow herself not to comfort me, but I understand her need to cry alone, her need to protect and shield those around her from the true extent of what she's feeling is something we share…I wish I was as strong as her, that I could say with utter truthfulness that I've never needed comfort from her and even been glad by her forceful refusal not to leave me when I do. The fact that my feelings are not under my control, that they're exaggerated and exacerbated by my illness, doesn't ease the guilt I bear when those feelings are shared and burdened onto others. When sharing your suffering only makes you feel worse, there is really only one other option left to you and that's to suffer it alone and hope that no one hears you.

I wrap my free arm around myself, holding tightly as with each sob I hear and with each jagged breath my aunt takes, the hollow cavern inside me deepens. This is my punishment, the retribution I must bear for the suffering I cause those around me. Masochistic though it may sound and masochistic though it may be, the perpetrators should always suffer more than the victims they harm. Still I hope, impossible though it may be, that she knows I'm here. As much as I admire, respect, understand and even appreciate her not crying before me, I sometimes wish that she would, just so I know that, in moments like these, it's ok to be weak.

Nearly ten minutes go by before my aunt stops crying completely. Then I hear the gentle thump of what I imagine to be her clothes falling onto the floor, a few seconds later and with my ear no longer against the wall, I hear the rubbery squeak of a foot moving across the bath tray where the shower hangs over it. I move away from the wall and lean against the bed for what feels like a long time, until the beeping of my phone makes me pull my reluctant body off the floor in the hunt for my phone. I locate it in the pocket of my jacket and I stare with bafflement at the screen which tells me I have three messages. Unaccustomed to such popularity and reminded of a time when I was, I click into the first message. It's from Sarah: *Hey! How was the appointment? I hope it went well. Thinking of you. Little sis xxx*

I quickly message her back saying that it was a waste of time and that we'd see her tomorrow. The next message is from Kate: *How did your appointment go?*

I send her a similar message to the one I sent Sarah, knowing that my aunt will phone her tomorrow when we get home. The last message is from Logan. I stare at his name on the top of the screen, relief surging through me. I should never have doubted him. I let my eyes glide over the short message but a message nonetheless: *Hi, did you have your second opinion today? How did it go?*

I eagerly write back that the doctors think I'm mad and need therapy, haha. My message is all very light and airy. I press send and go over to my bed, sitting on it and leaning against the plush pillows at my back, keen to hear his response while at the same time I'm both battered by resentment and engulfed in relief. I despise my habitual fear of losing the few friends I have left. I try to remember a time during which I didn't guard myself against them, when I didn't believe with certainty in the question of *when* they would leave but *if* they would, and a time when I didn't go over every meeting and conversation, looking for things I might have said or done wrong that might cause them to leave.

After a few minutes my phone beeps with another message from Logan: *If all the doctors are saying the same thing, then do you think they might be right? Therapy might be good for you; it's worth a try, isn't it?*

I read the message again, swallowing hard against the icy feeling in my gut. My eyes jar against each word as though they're unwilling to believe they're real. My heart is bouncing hard against my ribs, my organs feel bruised, blanched, and with each word that follows I feel the battery deepening. How can he say that after what he saw? Granted, I was far from my worst but surely he saw the potential of how bad things could get? How could he believe I was faking? I drop my phone onto the bed as though it's a poisoned apple as my aunt comes out of the bathroom, a towel wrapped around her head. She looks better. It's me who's broken now. I grab my nightclothes and go into the bathroom to change, the dense steam catching in my throat. I sit on the edge of the damp bath with my arms wrapped around me as though to contain my unravelling. The walls are so wet that streaks of water run down them like tears. I slowly release the breath I was unaware of holding, Logan's words far more damaging than any the doctors have said.

Chapter Fourteen

My aunt and I barely speak on the way home from Northcairn. The only thing keeping the tension at bay is the fact that our animosity isn't directed at each other but united against the same establishment that's labelled and tossed me aside.

I look at my aunt as the world beyond her window flashes by. My lips move as though to frame the first letter of the question I've been building myself up to ask, but instead they lock, refusing to utter it. My aunt's brown hair is tied in a messy bun and the bags under her eyes tell me she's slept as little as I did. I look away...I know there's no point in asking, I know she doesn't have the answer to what happens next, but the urge to ask nonetheless, to hear out loud and confirm that neither of us knows is compelling.

I want to know where my aunt who was readying herself for a fight went, where all the information and research vanished to. Has she grown as tired as I have, so ground down by the toil of this disease that she can't fight any further? And if so, then what hope is there for me?

We arrive home at about five o'clock. After saying hello to Sarah and Dog I head to my dining room under the pretence of having a nap. I change from my jeans into pyjama bottoms but

I don't bother changing my top; half-dressed, I feel I'm still part of the day. I cuddle under my blankets, the familiar smell and feel of them inviting. I shut my eyes, trying to rest, but the longer I lie there the more irritated and frustrated I become. The sheets tangle around my feet as I shift position yet again. I don't feel the same exhaustion now as I did in the car; it's as though my body's celebrating its return to my caged castle by throwing me a scrap of energy. I wish I could understand this illness's logic, its reason and rhythm. Exertion equals exhaustion, but when that exhaustion will come is its own private secret. An hour or so after? A week?... It lulls you into believing you've escaped its punishment, then it strikes hard and fast. You rally and think great! I'm ok, I can do this but then it snatches you, dragging you further down. You might think fatigue lies in the same place but we, the chronically unwell, can contradict you. Physical and mental exhaustion are individual: it's when the two collide that the damage is really done.

I get out of bed and take my phone from my jeans pocket before climbing back under the covers; I can hear my aunt and Sarah moving about the kitchen as they prepare dinner.

I use my phone to look up the blogs my aunt once talked about. It takes some searching but I do find them and once I find one, I find countless more. After reading three or four I can't deny the paralleled theme of my own experience any longer: previously healthy, outgoing and happy person's life is destroyed by an unknown illness; doctors are baffled; tests for everything come back normal; people are wrongly diagnosed (the doctors' favourites for erroneous diagnoses seem to be: ME/CFS, multiple sclerosis, lupus, mental illness, Alzheimer's, fibromyalgia, arthritis). The person's life worsens. The individual then finds a doctor who believes them (most of these sites are American, but by the sound of it people are paying a lot of money for that belief). The person's belief in the doctor and doctor's belief in the patient pay off, and the said person is diagnosed with Lyme disease. Countless tests are sent to laboratories around the world to prove it. Some sites don't go into the treatment because the person hasn't got that far, and I don't continue reading the ones that have. It doesn't feel relevant when I haven't been diagnosed with Lyme.

I begin to understand where my aunt's fight went, why she shrank in the doctor's chair and said little more...she knew there was no point. The appointment we had has been had by those before us. It's here in black and white, both print and metaphoric. Some doctors go so far as to say that Lyme disease doesn't even exist. Entire countries and governments downplay it by calling it rare, and many will admit it's in other countries but not their own. Whether I have it or not, Lyme is the dirty plague no one wants to admit to having. Why bury their heads? Why deny it when so many of the people in their countries have been diagnosed with it? Why should people have to leave their own country when they're so ill in order to get a diagnosis and treatment? Why do you call these people crazy and lazy, when it's you who's made them mad?

I stop reading the introduction to the blogs, skipping to the bits about the doctors instead. I know how much effort has gone into every letter that these people have typed but I can't stand to read how their lives have been destroyed, the pain and the suffering they and their families are going through. I understand why they wrote them; they want to make people understand the magnitude of what they've lost; they want everyone to know they weren't always this sick, crippled person; they need someone, anyone, to understand. They need a beginning to their story, a middle and at least the hope of an end.

***

The room around me is bathed in a golden glow from the light filtering through the curtains. I lie on my side, staring apathetically at the wall opposite me. I'm so tired, I don't understand. I don't know what to do. We only came home yesterday but it feels like days ago. I try to think of a reason for me to get out of bed, a single purpose or task…but there are none. This empty existence will continue as it has done for the last two and a half years, with little to break up its monotony. Nonetheless, I pull myself up into a sitting position and heave myself out of bed. I move slowly to the door and down the hall to the kitchen.

'Morning,' Sarah says brightly from the kitchen table where a number of textbooks are spread out across it.

'Hi,' I say. Caught off guard, I stop dead in my tracks, I hadn't prepared myself for having company.

'How you feeling?' Sarah asks, her pen swinging in between her fingers.

'Fine,' I lie. 'I thought your train was this morning?'

'I got the date mixed up, it's tomorrow morning,' she informs me.

I move to the kettle and turn it on.

'How are you?' I ask, more out of duty than interest.

'I'm great. I've got heaps to do for my coursework but oh well,' she says happily.

Her cheerfulness is annoying. I turn as the kettle automatically clicks off. It's only half-full but I struggle to lift it with one hand. I put it down to lift it with two hands but I hear the loud squawk of a chair leg, and the next thing Sarah's arm is reaching round me for the kettle's handle.

'I'll make that – you sit down. You were so busy yesterday,' she says.

I let her take the kettle from me, but I don't sit down. I won't be told what to do by my little sister. I'm not yet completely devoid of pride or independence. I go to the fridge and examine its contents for something to eat. I grab a block of cheese and what's left of the lettuce and take it to the worktop. I pull out a large knife and the chopping board. I need the long knife so that I can put my hand on both sides of the handle and blade. It's the only way I can get the knife to cut through the cheese. Even at that, my arms shake under the effort.

'Joyce, look, I can do it,' Sarah says hurriedly, taking the partly embedded knife from my hands. 'It's solid, isn't it?' she remarks, screwing up her face like it's a huge effort, even though with her hand the knife glides through the cheese with ease.

She's being nice, I remind myself: don't be mean when she's only trying to make you feel better.

'Thanks,' I say, hoping the mutter in my voice will hide my bitterness.

Normally, I would look upon her efforts with kindness, even amusement, but not today. I wasn't prepared for company; my mask's not in place and I don't have the energy to find it. I just wanted a day, after the intensity of being with my aunt in Northcairn, where I didn't have to pretend to be anything other than miserable. I want to go back into my bubble, where I can pretend that what I feel is what everyone feels and the only reason I'm home all day is because I've got a day off. Only Sarah and her healthy body that moves with such wondrous fluidity and strength keep bursting my make-believe.

'I'll bring it through to you,' Sarah says; the brightness that was there before has faded. She glances at me before reaching for the bread; she looks nervous.

I should have been nicer to her, I scold myself as I head down the hall to my dining room, using the walls to help me along. I hear footsteps behind me and I can't help but sigh with dread. Just leave me alone, I think silently. Sarah takes my other arm and I force myself to throw away my pride and smile gratefully so I don't upset her further. In my dining room Sarah helps me into the sofa bed; she props me up with pillows and tucks the covers around me like I did when she was the child.

'Are you comfy?' she asks.

No, I think tersely.

'Yeah,' I say quietly.

'You look a bit...' She does a strange wiggling motion as though she's lost her balance. '...Yeah I'll move this one. Is that better?'

No, now please go away.

'Yes.'

'Are you sure? I can't get more pillows.'

'It's fine.'

'Well, I don't want you to be fine...I want you to be comfy,' she says almost desperately, disappearing from my room and off up the stairs.

You can't make me comfy, I want to tell her – the discomfort is not on the outside.

'Sarah, it's fine,' I try to call after her, but I can't make my voice loud enough for her to hear. I wish she had left this morning; she's stressing me out and there's still an entire afternoon to go.

Sarah reappears with more pillows and puts them around and behind me. To be fair to her, I am more comfortable.

'Right, what else?' she says to herself. 'Ehm, phone, remote – do you need your laptop?' she asks as she puts my phone and the TV remote beside me.

'No,' I say shortly, wishing she would leave. I don't want to hurt her by being mean and I don't want to disappoint her by breaking down before her.

'Ok. I'll go get your tea or make you a new one. It's probably cold by now,' she says quickly, her movements jittery. 'Right, yeah, I'll be back in a minute.'

I listen, inwardly cringing at the clattering and banging going on in the kitchen. I want to know what she's doing; she's been gone for ages now. I want to make sure she's not making a mess that I'll have to clean up when she leaves tomorrow because let's face it – my aunt's not going to; she's never here long enough to care what state the cottage gets into. I'd forgotten how quiet my aunt has become because of me: she never slams the doors or blares the kitchen radio, she never stomps down the hall or shouts for Dog to come to her. I should remember to thank her tonight, I think to myself as Sarah bangs the back door and makes me jump.

I can tell by the way Sarah struggles to open the door that she's carrying a tray. When I see what's on it I can't help but soften towards her. She puts the tray on my lap and looks at me expectantly.

'Thank you,' I say, smiling gratefully.

A yellow rose from the garden sits on the tray in its own little vase beside my sandwich. Sarah hates roses, she has ever since she was a child and fell off her bike into a large rose bush. It's safe to say the rose bush was the victor: Sarah was scratched to pieces. I think she cried the whole way home. When Aunt Beth and I went outside to see what had happened, it was me Sarah ran to for comfort. Since then she doesn't even like touching them.

'It stabbed me, but I cut the thorn off so you'll be safe,' she says, holding out her thumb for me to look at, even though there's nothing to be seen.

I admire its petals as Sarah leaves my room and reappears a moment later with her own lunch and sits on my bed. I watch as she makes herself comfortable and I'm glad, for now, that she's here. We wouldn't be sisters if we weren't there at each other's side even if we'd rather, on odd days like these, be alone.

Chapter Fifteen

Top ten things the chronically ill must consider when going anywhere, and therefore, why the healthy shouldn't be allowed to get annoyed at the sick for being able to go to some events and not others.

- Is advance notice required? Because we, the sick, can't really RSVP when we don't know how we're going to feel tomorrow, never mind in a week's time.
- Casual or fancy? The more effort required to get ready, the more likely we'll use up all our energy getting prepared.
- Where is the event? Ten minutes away, doable. Twenty, getting less likely. Thirty, are you kidding? I'll arrive only to be too tired to enter.
- Is the building new or old? If it's old, then it's unlikely to have a lift or disabled access and far more likely to have those awkward, steep steps just to enter the building, never mind the possibility of ones inside.
- Is the event at the front or back of the building? How much walking is required just to get to it is a large factor.
- Will there be places to sit? Standing and I are not on the best of terms right now.
- Can I take my carer, I mean my aunty? Because she's kind

of my getaway driver. Speaking of driving…Can the car be parked by the entrance or can I be dropped off near the door? Because walking to the event and then having to attend the event may be asking too much of the old body.

• How many people will be there? The noise alone of a large group can overwhelm and drain, never mind if there's music involved. Will I know any of the people there?

• Is this event one I can slip out of without being noticed, or will the entire room stop to watch as I shuffle my way out? I've been to one of these and I have to say, being the main attraction wasn't as much fun as I imagined it might be.

• I know I've said this one before but I'll say it again because it's pretty important. How do we feel on the day? Can we cancel at the last minute without causing disruption or offence?

'Thanks for lunch,' I say to Sarah. 'Are you going to go and do your coursework?'

'Mhh,' Sarah mutters distractedly, smiling at whatever message has just come through on her phone.

'I think I'm going to stay in bed this afternoon.' I'm trying really hard not to be blunt here. I'm hoping she'll take the hint and go.

'Ok…' she says, her fingers moving as she sends a message back, '…so, what film do you want to watch?'

I watch as she peruses my DVD collection. Her presence shouldn't annoy me…but it does. I can't rest with her being in my room. I can't relax with anyone in the house because I don't know what's going to happen next, I can't predict and calculate the effect; it's as though my body's on tensed alert, waiting for something to happen for which it must be constantly prepared to take flight or fight.

I know I shall miss her company tomorrow, when she's not here to talk through the film as she is now, but I don't have the willpower to pretend to care about any of the things she's talking about. It's not her fault, though: I can't be irritated at her for wanting to spend time with me, even though that's what I feel, so I try, truly I do. I smile at her comments, I answer her questions with more than just a yes or a no, I resist the desire to snap at her when she asks me about Logan, and instead I reply with reframed politeness. I listen as she talks about her new boyfriend, the huge amount of work she has for college, her flatmates and work. And did I know my phone is flashing?

'It's Amy,' I tell Sarah, reading the message. 'She's having her eighteenth next week.'

'Oh. Do you think you can go?' Sarah asks awkwardly, pulling the blankets over her feet.

'No, probably not.'

'You should talk to Beth. She might be able to take you. I'm sure she wouldn't mind being on call if you needed to leave early or something.'

"Something" meaning me needing to be carried out of the building.

'It's at the steading,' I say, pulling the covers off me to cool myself down.

The steading is a beautiful old building, with lots of fun little doors and passageways, hidden rooms and plenty of uneven stairs dating back to the 17th century.

'Oh, never mind. I'm sure she'll have another party for her twenty-first. You'll be well by then,' she informs me with unquestioning optimism.

***

Sarah abandoned me for Aunt Beth when she came home from work. I ate dinner alone in my dining room, glad of the stillness. After a few hours I get up to take my plate to the kitchen. Despite it being empty, my heightened senses can still smell the food that had been on it and the lingering smell is far less enjoyable than when it had first arrived.

I put the plate by the sink, wondering where Sarah and Aunt Beth are: when I passed the sitting room there was no sound from within. I haven't seen Dog either but I'm sure they would have told me if they were taking him out. I move slowly to the back door; I bend down to put on my shoes but then discard them; I don't really need them and they take too long to put on for the irrational panic that's beginning to swell in my stomach. Where are they?

As soon as I open the door I can see them: they're sitting on the bench at the patio only a few feet away, enjoying the last of the evening's sunshine. I've been trapped inside so long I had barely noticed summer's arrival. Dog's at the end of the garden, sniffing the grass around the base of a great oak tree. I'm not sure if I should join them: now that I'm here the evening seems inviting, a tantalising calm with a melody of birdsong. I'm still debating when Sarah speaks.

'She seemed fine today. Well, she was tired…I had to help her into bed,' Sarah says as though in answer to a question I never heard.

I wrap one of my arms around my ribs. I don't think her comment's fair: I was doing just fine on my own, like I have been for nearly two and a half years. I didn't want her help, I didn't need it; yet I know deep down that I often do.

'Did she mention her appointment?' Aunt Beth asks.

The bench is angled so that I can only see part of Sarah's side and only the back of Aunt Beth.

'No,' Sarah says like a spy reporting to her master.

'I'm not sure if I should take her to CBT or not,' Aunt Beth says, her words like swooping gulls in my gut.

'I can't believe they think it's in her head...' Sarah says with indignation but when she speaks next her voice is clogged with emotion. '...How can it be in her head?'

'The mind's very powerful. Look at those people with OCD or, huh, I don't know, schizophrenia,' Aunt Beth says, sighing heavily and putting a comforting arm around Sarah's shoulders.

'You don't think it's in her head, do you?' Sarah asks.

Dog barks with excitement and comes running over as he notices me standing in the doorway. Without realising it I've been clinging onto the door frame with my other hand to keep me upright. My stiffened fingers are reluctant to let go in order for me to stroke Dog's head.

'Joyce,' my aunt sounds alarmed as they both turn to look at me.

I don't look at her. I look at Dog, my only ally. I don't think I can move. Fight or flight – they always seem to ignore the third... freeze. In my head I try to think of all the animals that take this stance, I know there are a lot, I've seen them in documentaries on TV, but the only one I can think of is mice. I feel a strange affiliation to these little creatures, picked on and played with by those higher in the pecking order, then either tossed aside or devoured when the fun's passed.

'Well, do you think it's all in my head?' I ask, my heart beating worryingly hard. I look up at my aunt and Sarah, waiting for the answer.

'…No, of course I don't,' Aunt Beth says strongly.

Without a word I turn and go to my dining room and in the passing hours that I hunt for that rare thing called sleep, my mind is plagued and besieged by words that deepen my doubt. Over and over again, they come at different angles, changing time and rhythm to see which mantra will sound worst.

Might never get better. Psychological elements. Are you saying this is all in my head? Therapy might be good for you.

Chapter Sixteen

Question: what's the worst thing you can do to someone who is chronically ill?

Answer: make them feel they need to prove how ill they are.

Their remarks haunt me in the days that come, lingering in the shadows of my mind; they attack me in the quiet moments when my guard is lowered, refusing to be forgotten or ignored.

My past, my present and my lost future swirl around my mind as I lie in my bed upstairs, the warm summer sun clashing with the morbidity festering inside me. I grab my phone from beside my bed and consider the message Amy sent me about her eighteenth, remembering a time when such an invitation would be a reason for joy rather than guilt and of the days when I celebrated rather than ignored my own birthday.

'What do you call that?' the instructor's son/apprentice calls to us mockingly.

I try to shout something back but I'm laughing too hard.

'You lot over there, paddle forwards to turn around,' he calls from inside his canoe. He's not much older than us, blond-haired, blue-eyed and athletically built.

I never thought we would get to come to the activity centre for my fifteenth birthday but somehow Aunt Beth found the money. She couldn't afford for us to come for the whole day so we're here for the afternoon instead.

There are ten of us on the makeshift raft we had to build from scratch. It took an embarrassing amount of time to construct and the first attempt fell apart and saw several of us swimming across the loch-sized pond to retrieve the drums and wooden beams that fell off and floated away. We try and do what the guy instructed but we end up going sideways. There are shouts from behind me as the girls at the back try to stay on as the raft bumps and gets stuck in the embankment. The aim of the game is to row to one side of the pond and back again in under ten minutes…so far we're on eighteen. With lots of kicking and pushing of our legs and oars we manage to get back onto the water and into the middle of the pond.

'Show off!' Amy shouts jovially at the guy who comes gliding towards us in his canoe: he's standing up and steering towards us without effort.

'What was that?' he calls, stopping a short distance away. He lifts his oar and brings it down on the surface of the pond, showering us with cold pond water.

Many of the girls who are still dry duck behind those who aren't, while we try and splash him back, with pitiful results.

'What did you say?' the guy calls.

'Show off!' Amy, Rebecca and I yell back, still trying to splash him.

'What was that?' he calls again gliding towards us and putting his oar in the water as he goes sailing past, sending a wave of water over all of us.

Everyone yells and laughs; Aunt Beth and the instructor who are standing at the edge of the pond are laughing, too.

'Joy!' Rebecca calls as I jump off the raft and nearly unbalance everyone else.

My life jacket stops me from dipping beneath the water. I swim towards the guy, slowed and hampered by the thickness of my life jacket which cuts into my neck and under my arms.

'Joy, his phone,' my aunt shouts in a panic as I reach his canoe.

'Have you got anything in your pockets?' I ask, the water lapping over

the rim of my life jacket.

'No,' he says giving me an odd look.

'Great,' I say enthusiastically, grabbing the edge of the canoe and pulling myself up with it like a push-up bar and then letting go so the canoe rocks back and forth.

'Oh no, no, no, no,' the guy panics but manages to keep his balance. 'Don't you dare!'

'Sorry, what did you say?' I ask innocently as the girls on the raft start chanting J-O-Y, J-O-Y, J-O-Y.

This time I put all my weight onto the edge of the canoe before letting go. The guy wobbles, keeps his balance…and then falls face first into the water beside me. Everyone cheers and hits the water with their oars, not caring if they get wet or not. Once the guy recovers from his spluttering and laughing, he helps me pull Amy and everyone else into the water.

It was one of the best birthdays I've ever been to and certainly the best one of mine.

With a heavy sigh I send Amy a message, saying that I really want to come but I'm not sure how I'll be feeling on the day, and that I don't think it's likely I'd be able to come. My tired mind ponders over the spelling of the words, the letters that I'm thinking of aren't always the letters that I type, creating incoherent words and sentences. Words that were once written without thought now need careful consideration, my mind hesitating with uncertainty over things that were once sure. *Mental barriers! Therapy!*

I get out of bed, head downstairs and make myself something to eat. *Are you saying this is all in my head? I'd asked. Yes, Dr Burk replies, the simple words slice my insides.*

I go back upstairs and sit on my bed, rubbing my aching neck. *The mind is very powerful!* I look up and catch my reflection in the mirror and for the first time in months I don't look away,

I get up and sit before it, studying my face. There's nothing there that screams out illness, there's nothing obvious for people or doctors to see – not for those who never knew me before I was ill. But I see them, the marks this illness has left. The hollowed and darkened marks around my eyes are not prominent but they were never there before. My face is reddened from a recent hot flush that left me uncomfortably sweaty. I lean in closer to examine my eyes, the colour faded from them, and the bright whites are dull and tainted grey, cracked with a couple of thin red lines. My auburn hair is still glossy but the ends are thick with splits. It's been years since I had it professionally cut. A noisy and busy hairdresser's is far from inviting when you're chronically ill, so the task of cutting my hair falls on my aunt's shoulders like so many other things. Beyond that there's nothing to tell a stranger of my ill health. *You don't think it's in her head, do you? my sister had asked.*

'I don't know you,' I say out loud. Watching my mirrored reflection moving, too.

Psychological elements!

'I don't understand what's happened,' I say, my heart beating hard. I know what happened, I experienced it all...but I don't understand. It's too much, the grief and the loss are too huge to be contemplated or understood.

Therapy might be good for you. Logan's message repeats in my head.

The betrayal's too cutting for my mind and body to let me feel. *Help you overcome the mental barriers which are stopping you from getting better. Dr Careless's voice whispers viciously amidst the jumble of voices of my memory.*

'I don't want this,' I say, my body rigid. 'I'm not crazy, I'm not imagining it, I'm not crazy.'

Might never get better!

I lean forwards and put my head in my hands, rocking back and forth.

Are you saying this is all in my head? Yes. Psychological elements. Therapy might be good for you. Mental barriers.

I look up, breathing hard. I stagger to my feet and throw open the wardrobe doors, furiously pulling out its contents until I find my old sports clothes. I put them on and am momentarily engulfed in the smell of my old self, which is sweetly soft. I want to take them off to keep the smell treasured but I remind myself I have to do this to find Joy.

I head downstairs and put on my old running trainers. Like my clothes, they haven't been worn in two and a half years and they have to be searched for. The feel of the laces as I tie them is so nostalgic and comforting it's like I'm her again, sixteen and full of life, it's like she's calling home. I go out the front door and shut it behind me. I can hear Dog barking from within but this time I must go alone.

I walk towards the end of the drive with determination but as I near the road my anxiety grows. How long has it been since I left the house alone? Certainly it was before I was ill. The boundary of my compound feels safe: the world beyond it lurking with danger and ill omens. I would have drawn up the drawbridge long ago had it not been made of tar and gravel. The world around me lengthens as the drive opens up to the world that's vast, daunting and unknown. Yet I know I know it.

Despite the tightness in my gut I turn left and set off on a quick walk, building my pace until I break out into a running jog. After a few strides of disbelief, I start to smile: I'm running, I'm actually running! My feet bounce off the road with each step, my arms swing, full of power to propel me forwards. I can feel energy coursing through me, the cool air gliding over me as supple as water. I'm going to run to the loch, I suddenly decide with joyous zeal, I'll swim in its silky waters and float on its surface with the soft clouds of the sky and the birds dancing above me. I keep running: Joy's within my sights.

I'm not sure how long I run for. I used to listen to music to judge how long I'd been out for, but I was in such a rush I'd not taken any. In my head I sing every song I can think of, to get my body to move to its rhythm the way it used to, but it's not working – my body's ailing. Every step is depleting me, my heart is pounding painfully loud in my ears and every muscle, tissue, cell and bone within me is begging for me to stop. I don't hear the maturing lambs bleating or their mothers' answering cries or the twittering of the birds. I don't see the green fields lined by fences and drystone walls or the hedges or trees. I see only the road in front of me as one foot overtakes the other. My arms have become nothing more than ineffective and cumbersome. My pace slows to a bouncy walk, my feet barely coming off the ground.

My left foot drags out behind me, the toe scraping along the road. I fall fast and hard. I can't move my arms fast enough to protect my face but I do manage to turn it in time so my chin doesn't smash into the road. My cheek and jawline hit the road like cheese through a grater. I lie still, my face smarting, my heart aching under its ferocious pounding. I lie on the road until the beating of my heart doesn't hurt my ears anymore. Then I stretch out my arm in front of me and use my legs to drag myself forwards like a soldier approaching enemy lines. I have to keep moving. I don't give in. I won't give up, I cannot surrender. I crawl on my stomach – I don't know for how long but the effort is stupendous, and when I look behind me I've barely moved more than a metre.

I let out a strangled cry of frustration and desperation as Joy slips further and further away. I'm not too proud to beg for her…if only she still existed. I have to stand up, I order myself, but my body's so tired that it doesn't care about what I want. It's the only way, I cajole, you have to overcome your barriers, the psychological elements, this is the only way, you must push through it, you have to break free and then everything will be better. You won't hurt anymore, you won't hurt anyone, you'll be free. Don't we all deserve to be free?

I pull my knee up to the side of my chest and then rock from side to side until my knee is under me, and then I do the same with my other knee so that both knees are under my chest. I use my fragile arms to lift up my torso and then I leave them extended, the weight of my upper body upon their hollow weakness. I heave my backside up into the air like a bizarre yoga pose, but my knees lock halfway. Gritting my teeth against the strain upon them, I push my legs with all my might to try and straighten them, but I can't. I can see my legs tremble through my loose trousers, as visible as it feels, and it reminds me of the time before I had the sofa bed, when the dining room still held a table and when I had to battle most nights to get up the stairs. My legs would shake so severely that the fabric of my school trousers would tremble and my aunt would have her arms around me to help me and she'd tell me that everything would be all right. I don't know how she got me up those stairs. I think she all but carried me….only she's not here now and she stopped saying long ago that everything would be all right.

I feel my aching frame swaying with fatigue; I try to counter it, but my weight sways onto my left leg. I can feel it warning me what will happen, but it happens long before I can do anything to rectify my leg giving out from under me. Pain shoots up my knee as it crashes down onto the road and scrapes out from under me, my body falling sideways onto the sloping verge which slides and rolls me downwards. I try to grab at the long chunks of grass but my movements are too slow. I feel myself falling, it can't be far but it feels in that moment like the sensation could last forever. I land face up in the ditch. My blood coursing through me with the weight of liquid lead. The weight of my body smothers me. Making me feel like I might sink deep into the mud, to be unearthed thousands of years later like a bog body that will be examined and marvelled over by the medical profession with more care and respect than was ever given to me in life. Time is immeasurable. The darkness tempting. The soft clouds of the sky and the birds dance above me.

Chapter Seventeen

Beth.

There are no lights on in the cottage as I park the car in the drive, my headlights shining off its white walls until I turn the engine off and I'm plunged into darkness. When I step out of the car, I hesitate, the quiet stillness of the cottage eerie in the darkening of the summer's night. I shut the car door as quietly as I can and head into the cottage through the back door. In the darkness of the kitchen I hear a high-pitched whimper and I hasten to turn on the light, my hands scrabbling over the wall until they find and turn on the switch – Dog sits by the closed door which leads into the hall; he looks at me and then to the door before whimpering once more.

'What is it?' I say, more to myself than to Dog.

I push him out of the way and go into the hall, my body rigid: Joyce always has Dog with her, but maybe she's sleeping, I tell myself to calm my quickening heart. I peer into her new bedroom but the room's in complete darkness. I move back into the hall and turn on the light beside her room before opening her door wider and peering inside.

'Joyce?' I say gently in case she's asleep.

Silence. I open the door a little wider so the light from the hall creeps up over the covers of the sofa bed which slowly rise in the shape of a body. I don't open the door any wider – I don't want the light to reach her face and potentially wake her. I carefully shut the door of her room and head back to the kitchen. Shutting the kitchen door behind me, I'm relieved but still unable to shake the ill feeling Dog's whimpering has instilled inside me.

Dog clambers about my legs as I go to the cupboard and pull out a bottle of wine. I pour myself a glass, then grab a sheet of writing paper and a pen from the drawer before moving to the table.

'Dog,' I say impatiently as he tangles himself about my legs.

I sit down and take a deep sip of wine, enjoying the way it glides down my throat like liquid gold. Then I take up my pen and write.

Dear Mum and Dad

I hope life is more peaceful with you. Things here have been hard since we came back from Northcairn. I'm trying to be cheerful and act like nothing has changed but I think she can tell, I think she knows there's nowhere left to go and that I don't know what to do. There are no more roads to go down. It's just us. I don't know how to help her; I keep trying but it's getting harder and harder to do.

When I came home at the start of the week and Joyce came in, I asked how she was and she said, 'I'm f-f-f...' It was like she was physically choking on the word, trying desperately to get it out. I think everything inside of her is out of sync, it's as though she's trying frantically to dance to a tune that's constantly changing. '...Fin, fars, farn, fine.' When she finally said it, she looked so sad and alone. She just stood there, staring at nothing. I wanted to go to her and hug her. If it had been Sarah or Kate then I wouldn't have hesitated but she isn't, she's Joyce.

I wish I could say the week improved, that I improved, but I'd just had enough. I never know what I'm coming home to. Joyce's mood...

I pause, sighing heavily. I sip and continue.

...can be changeable, she can get grumpy and snappy at times, she gets spells of being very low, worryingly so, but mostly she smiles. But that night she was quiet and I was tired. I went into the sitting room and I saw the closed curtains and I just had had enough so I pulled them open. I turned up the TV and when she asked if she could turn it down, I told her I was watching the programme. I remember she was sitting at an awkward angle so that she was shaded from the light. After a moment or two she got up and went to her new room (the old dining room: remember I told you how we changed it into a bedroom for her?). I felt terrible. She'd been on her own all day and all she wanted to do was sit beside me. I know the light hurts her, I've read all about the glare being blinding and Joyce always wears sunglasses, even when she's just popping out for a moment. I've read it makes their eyeballs painful, by the sound of it, it's like a huge pressure in their eyes. It can cause headaches and goodness knows... Joyce gets enough of those. And the noise: Joyce once told me it reverberates in her head and that some/most tones feel like someone stabbing a needle through her ear and into her brain. Was what I did any better than abuse? I knew it would hurt her, but I did it anyway. Even when she sat there after I opened the curtains, she never said anything, she was willing to sit in pain just to be in my company, but then I made that pain unbearable by turning up the TV.

I take another sip, rubbing my forehead to try and drown out Dog's whining.

I wish you were here, Mum, you always know what to do. I did go through to her room later on and asked if I could join her. 'You won't be able to hear,' she told me. She never said it with anger or sadness, she simply said it, which in a way was worse. All I wanted to do was shut the door and leave but I told her I wanted to stay. I sat beside her and put my arm around her. She turned the volume up – I still couldn't really hear but I presume it was the highest she could stand it being. It took fifteen minutes before her body relaxed into me, I don't know if it was because she felt it or because her body was fatigued but it was nice to sit with her. I've come to realise that you were right, Dad, when you always told me to appreciate the good moments when they happen and memorise them (that's why I'm telling you about this now), so that they can sustain you through the bad ones. I was content in that moment, even when discord surrounded us.

Your daughter,

Beth.

I fold the letter and wipe my damp cheeks. Dog's sitting at the side of the chair, looking up at me imploringly.

'What is it?' I ask him.

He jumps up and paws at my arm – his claws sharp on my bare skin.

'Hey...' I say, pushing him down. '...Stop.'

I get up to check his food and water bowl...but they're full. I turn back around and it's then that I see Joyce's phone on the worktop. Joyce always has her phone with her; it's a little obsessive the way she carries it at all times but she got quite a fright when she collapsed in the house alone. I stare at it for a horrible moment, frozen to the spot, and then I run down the hall and open her door as wide as it will go. I try to be as quiet as I can in my haste to cross her room and as I feel for her absent body amongst the covers which were pulled back as though she were there. I turn on the light, just to confirm what I already know. Then I run up the stairs and turn on her bedroom light to find it empty, too, her wardrobe doors open and the contents flung around the room. I check my room, I check every room...she's gone.

'Joyce?' I call out, trying not to panic. 'Joyce!'

I clasp the top of my head as though it will somehow focus my mind and inform me what I should do. I run to the kitchen and grab her phone. It takes me a while to figure out how to work it, but I manage to get into her contacts. I find who I'm looking for and press call…no answer, I try again and again.

'Hello?' he answers.

'Logan?' I say hastily.

'Yes.'

'It's Beth, Joyce's aunt. Is she with you?'

'Erm…' Logan pauses. I know teenagers and young people well enough to know when one's trying to figure out if they should cover for the other.

'Logan, she's missing. I have her phone, I don't know where she is or how long she's been gone,' I say, as inspiration comes to me and I search around the kitchen and hall for a note where we usually leave them. 'There's no note,' I say despondently to myself.

'She's not with me – I've not heard from her since she was in Northcairn,' he confesses. 'Do you want me to drive around, see if I can find her?'

'Yes. Please phone me if you find her.' I don't think I even said goodbye before I hung up.

I pace back and forth: I don't know what to do. Dog's gone ominously quiet. I grab my car keys and race to the car, the gravel tugging and kicking out from under my tyres as I head out of the drive. Left or right? Which way would she have gone? I turn right. I switch on my full beam lights and peer through the windscreen which is smattered with rain – the seat belt tight across my neck as I lean forwards. She can't have gone far; I know people say that, but truly Joyce can't have. Still, her stubbornness to persevere can be surprising but it can't override her illness, if it could…she would have been better years ago.

Every branch that sways in the corner of my eye makes me

slam on the brakes, every sheep moving about the tall grass is her struggling to stand, every set of rabbits' eyes reflecting off my lights are her eyes. I stop every hundred yards and lower the window to call her name into the strengthening rain, but no call is ever returned. I think of her lying somewhere, unconscious or unable to move, and my insides go cold with the thought of her waiting for me to come and find her. How long has she been waiting? Why was I not there? Why am I never there?

'Joyce,' I whisper repeatedly as I drive, until my voice becomes as desperate as the Dog's whimper.

Chapter Eighteen

It lied to me...that figure in a dark and hooded cloak, or perhaps it was the myth surrounding its legend that made me believe the pain would end and the suffering would stop. For surely this dark place of pain is purgatory and the distant and inaudible voices around me are the voices of other lost souls.

My hourglass of a body is most certainly lying down on its back because the sand is spread evenly against the back of my body; the parts of me which face upwards are tauntingly light, and my muddled mind struggles to tell where my skin ends and the air around me begins. I try to lift my head but the weight in it is overpowering; it presses into the back of my skull, pushing me into the darkness.

Something itches on my arm; it's growing in intensity the more aware I become of it and the more I become aware, the more it pulls my mind from the haze. I move a stiffened finger... then another. Slowly I drag my right arm across my body to my left arm. With sluggish and fumbling movements, I feel my arm until I get to the source of the itch. I feel the thing in my arm...I know I know what it's called...a top, tub, tip, type...something, I know it's called something. I know the thing it's connected to is a needle and the culprit of the itching is the fabric tape which holds it in place to the inside of my elbow. My fingers move clumsily to the corner of the tape and attempt to peel it away.

'Hey...' says a gentle voice. I hear its owner move and then a warm hand carefully takes my arm and places it back at my side. '...It's ok, you have a tube thing in your arm.'

I want to protest – it took a lot of effort to move my arm but I can't find the willpower to do so and I'm distracted by disappointment when the warm hand is removed from my arm: taking with it the warmth that had radiated down to my habitually chilled bones. I'm not sure how long I lie there, conscious of my unconsciousness but the itching has at least waned now I know what's causing it. When I manage to open my eyes, the world around me is nothing more than a mass of blurred colours. After a time, the shape of a room begins to appear. There's a light over the bed whose head has been pointed away from me. The corners of the room are shrouded in darkness, and sitting in a high-backed chair in the half-light beside my bed is Logan, with his head resting back against the chair and his eyes closed – he could be a child.

I slowly take in the hospital room: the IV in my arm and the white plastic clip on the end of my finger, which tells the machine that my heart is beating at 93 beats per minute. I must be really sick, I think to myself, to be in a room on my own.

'Joy?' Logan asks hesitantly.

I look at him. His brown hair is pressed down at the side where his head rested against the chair, his face is pale and tired-looking, his eyes groggy with sleep.

'How you feeling?' he asks.

I move my dry tongue around my mouth, trying to gather enough saliva to swallow so that I can speak.

'Here,' Logan says, springing to his feet and disappearing

from my sight. He reappears with a plastic cup but then pauses to consider my low position before fiddling with something at the side of the bed. The next thing I know, the part of the bed supporting my back is rising upward, along with my pulse which rises to 110. Logan goes to hand me the cup before thinking better of it and instead he holds it to my lips.

I hate drinking out of cups that other people hold for you. They're either too enthusiastic and pour the contents down you while you try desperately to drink quickly enough to prevent it – risking you choking, or they do the opposite and you end up drinking far less than the person holding the cup believes you have – leaving you thirsty. It provides you with the prospect of being drowned or dehydrated.

'Oh, sorry,' Logan says as the water overflows the sides of the cup and runs down my face and neck. 'Do you want more?'

'Mh,' I murmur. My throat's so dry that it's burning; the first few gulps of water hurt to swallow but slowly the pain goes as I near the end of the cup's contents.

'How are you feeling?' he asks again, when I finish the cup.

'Fi-ne,' I say, my voice cracking.

'Really?' he says sceptically, sitting on the edge of his seat, the cup clasped between his hands. 'Because you look terrible.'

'So do you,' I say sluggishly.

'Thought it might make you feel better if there was someone uglier in the room,' he says with a smile. 'I had to work hard to look this bad, you know: not even my dad could pull off wearing a hospital gown.'

I smile feebly.

'Where's…my aunt?' I ask.

'She's with one of the doctors, they're looking through your

notes to see if they can find anything that has been overlooked....
Joy, what happened, what were you doing?'

I look into the dark corner of the room as I remember
hunting for my running clothes, the sound of Dog barking as I
left him behind, running and then collapsing into the ditch.

'How far did I get?' I ask slowly.

'What?'

'How far?' I ask again, with a heavy sigh.

'Em, I'm not sure...maybe less than half a mile down the
road. Joy, what were you doing?' he asks anxiously.

I don't answer, I just stare into the gloom...the idea that I
could have run to the loch is pitiful now.

'Joy...' Logan almost whispers, '...you could have died.
They were talking about intubating you, you were dehydrated and
hypothermic, you had a blanket that looked like it belonged to a
spaceship just to try and regulate your temperature.'

He leans in and moves his hands as though to take mine, but
instead he thinks better of it and runs his hand through his hair –
lifting it and then flattening it back down.

'Were-were you...What were you doing?' he asks, his face
tensed with worry.

The question hangs between us like a physical cord, binding
the asker and the answerer together. Finally I answer, my voice
quietened by tired dejection. 'Proving...it's not...in my head.'

'....What, your illness?' Logan blurts after a moment's
thought. I look at him, remembering what he said.

'Even...' I take another breath, trying to get the words out,
'...you thought–I needed...therapy.'

'No, no that's not what I meant,' Logan says fervently. 'Joy,
I never–.'

The door into the room opens and a nurse in a dark blue uniform walks in with a clear IV bag in his hand. He pauses and smiles when he sees I'm awake.

'My name's Owen, I'm the nurse in charge,' he says, coming towards the bed. 'We met earlier but don't worry if you can't remember – you were just coming round at the time. I have to change your IV, if that's all right. Your friend can stay, though... if you want.'

He glances at me and then at Logan, perhaps sensing the tension between us, the clear bag of liquid suspended in his hand.

'Joy?' Logan asks with uncertainty but I can't answer; I'm scared of the hurt he'll hear in my voice if I do. 'Joy?...I'll-I'll go.'

I don't look up until he's at the door of the room. I watch his back disappear from view as the door shuts behind him. The room feels empty without him, even though, with the nurse changing my bag, there are the same number of people in it.

'What's that for?' I ask.

'You were dehydrated so your electrolytes were knocked off balance. This will help to fix them,' he says, checking the fluid is feeding through the tubes correctly. 'Can I get you anything?' he asks, looking at his pager.

'No thanks,' I reply meekly.

'Ok,' he says distractedly, putting his pager back in his pocket and leaving the room.

It's Aunt Beth who's sitting in the high-backed chair when I wake next. She's staring vaguely at the arm of the chair, her brows furrowed as though she's contemplating some great decision. Her elbow's resting on the arm of the chair with her hand covering her mouth as if to contain a cry within it.

'Aunt Beth,' I say quietly.

She jumps in her seat, her eyes darting to mine.

'Hi,' she says softly. 'Logan said you were more awake this time. How are you feeling?'

'Fine,' I say. Aunt Beth nods as though she knows exactly what I mean.

'Are you ok?' I ask.

Aunt Beth doesn't answer; instead she nods her head, her eyes welling with tears. She hastily pulls a tissue from her pocket and turns her face away from me to blow her nose, taking an unusually long time to clean it. Her eyes are clear of tears when she turns back around but her eyelashes are clumped together from wetness.

'Logan said you were talking to the doctor,' I state, saying the first thing that comes into my mind.

'Yes,' Aunt Beth says, resting her hand on my arm and rubbing her thumb back and forth along it. 'I read through your notes with the doctor...the whole way through it, it only mentions about five or six of your symptoms; they've ignored all your other ones.'

'Why?' I ask.

'I don't know, Joyce. Perhaps because they went against the ME and CFS diagnosis...I-I don't know,' she says with a heavy sigh. She looks exhausted, heavy bags shadow her once-vibrant eyes.

I watch her thumb as it moves back and forth across my arm. I know it's meant to be a kind and comforting gesture, but I wish I could tell her to stop because it feels like she's running a fine wire brush across my arm – its sharp, needle-like points stabbing deep into the tissue under my skin, and I have to resist my body's urge to flinch away.

'The doctor was nice, he spent his lunch hour with me so

that we could read through it all…' Aunt Beth pauses as though she's unsure of how to continue. '…I'm not sure he's allowed to but he gave me the name of a private hospital that specialises in Lyme disease. I gave them a call and they said they would get back to me.'

'We can't afford private treatment,' I say, my heart racing.

'It's all right. I'll find a way,' Aunt Beth says quickly, her eyes flooding with tears as she glances at the monitor which reads my pulse. 'It's not that different to paying my taxes to pay for hospitals and GPs.' I'm not sure who she's trying to convince more. 'It will all be fine, don't worry.'

I clasp her hand in mine and we sit still for a long time: both of us trying to be as strong as the other. But worry, its sister of anxiety, its brother of fear and its parent of all that could go wrong, is this disease's greatest corrupter of the mind and body.

***

I was discharged from hospital the following day. The doctor wanted to keep me in but he explained that with the improvement in my electrolyte balance, he couldn't justify keeping me in a room to myself. The idea of going into a ward where I would need assistance getting down to the bathroom filled me with dread. I couldn't stand the idea of everyone being able to see me and watch me as I struggled. I knew the noise and movements of patients, nurses, doctors, cleaners, porters, relatives and visiting friends all going past my bed would keep me clutched in a state of perpetual anxiety. And, in the quietness of night I would have nothing to distract my mind from the fear of the people around me, who might creep out of bed and attack me in my sleep. As irrational and ridiculous as it might sound, even to me, these possibilities are very real to a mind which habitually hunts for any possible danger, be it a broken paving stone I could trip on or the car my aunt will crash each time she uses it. The part of my mind still controlled by me does try to dismiss and diminish such ideas, but it's a waning power in contrast to the dominance of my ill mind.

So we came home and I've been sleeping downstairs for the past four days that I've been out of hospital. Summer's afternoon sun glows through the thick lining of my closed curtains, and the chatter of the birds in the garden overpowers the low volume of my TV. Every so often I can hear the gritty thud of Aunt Beth's trowel as she weeds the front garden and I imagine Dog by her side, watching with his head tilted to one side as though inspecting her work, or bounding about her as he so often does when she gardens – excited by the weeds and sticks being thrown into the wheelbarrow.

Aunt Beth informed me this afternoon that she managed to get an appointment for the private hospital. I'd presumed because it was private that we wouldn't have to wait to see the specialist, but the appointment's a month away and that's only because we managed to get a cancellation.

My thumb moves clumsily over the keys on my phone as I type a reply to Sarah. Every morning I've woken to find a message from her asking how I am. Throughout the day she will constantly message me; even when I think there can surely be nothing left to say, she will still find something to talk about – yesterday it was whether or not she should dye her hair. She spaces her messages out, leaving long periods of time between them so that she can speak to me throughout the day. I tried ignoring her at one point but she panicked and called the house phone to get Aunt Beth to check on me. I know she desperately wants to come home, but her new summer job in a school club programme won't allow it. I had hoped my trip to hospital could have stayed a secret but apparently my aunt's moral compass wouldn't allow her to hide such a thing from Sarah and Kate. Kate's not as bad as Sarah: she does message me once or twice a day, but once she ascertains that I'm alive she discontinues the conversation.

I'm trying to decide whether to watch the next episode or to attempt to read some of my book, when my phone sounds. It's from Logan: *Hey, so I had an interesting/awkward conversation with the Italian guy who now occupies your hospital bed! The nurse told me you'd been discharged. Is it ok if I come round on my way back from the hospital?*

His message reminds me that I never replied to the message he sent the other day. I quickly reply that I'm not well enough to see anyone; I add an apology for good measure, after he's driven all the way to the hospital for no reason...I feel a bit guilty. I begin the next episode, despite the aching in my head; I'd rather the pain than to hear my thoughts in the silence.

My phone beeps another message. Logan: *Yeah, of course, no problem. Listen, when I said before about therapy I never meant that I thought your illness was in your head. I never realised that's what they were wanting you to go for. I thought it was just someone for you to talk to which I thought would be good because you never talk about it to me, you tell me about your appointments and things but you never talk about what it's like or how you're really doing. Maybe that's my fault you don't, but either way I'm sorry I hurt you.*

I read the message a few times because my brain keeps missing parts; at first I thought it was the message that didn't make sense but clearly it's me. I don't know if I believe him. I don't know when I became someone who mistrusts everything and everyone – including myself. I don't believe the ground beneath my feet won't disappear, that the stairs I climb won't collapse, that the stranger walking past me won't harm me, or that those who are meant to help won't hurt me. I can't trust what my body feels or what my brain thinks…I'm lost and there's no peace in the unknown.

I sigh heavily, my body flushing hot, the thud-thud of my aunt's trowel in the background to my thoughts.

Me: *Ok.*

Logan: *Ok?*

Me: *Yeah, it's ok.*

Logan: *Can we meet up when you're feeling better?*

Me: *Ok.*

Logan: *Is that your new word of the week?*

I smile at the screen – I can't help it.

Me: *Hah, no.*

Logan: *That's a shame, it's a step up from fine!*

I shake my head as the smile on my face begrudgingly grows, despite the tight tug of the healing graze upon my cheek.

Me: *Thanks! Bye.*

Chapter Nineteen

Things that sick people would really appreciate for you to do and not do:

- Don't wave your hand in front of my face as you walk past me because I walk with a stick and wear dark sunglasses…I'm not blind, you nitwit.
- Huff and puff and then shove your way past me when I'm obviously disabled in some way or other – can't you just say 'excuse me' and then give me a moment to get out of the way. It's not like I enjoy being this slow. Also, if you knock me to the ground are you going to help me up and tend to whatever injury you've inflicted? I don't think so.
- Letting me skip the line or take your seat – I would personally like to thank all the people who do this; we might be so flustered that we can't thank you at the time but I assure you, you have saved us a great deal of exertion and pain. Your kindness does not go unnoticed.
- Do look where you're going – as much as you might enjoy tripping on my wheelchair and falling onto my lap…I assure you the feeling's not mutual, although it is highly amusing.
- Don't try and figure out what's wrong with me – seriously, you people aren't subtle. If you condition me, I will

condition you and you people all have the same condition, it's called IIM: insensitive, ignominious moron.

- A stranger's smile – being out and about is terrifying but I can't emphasise more what a simple smile from a stranger does to change an outing from being a horrible experience to being an ok one. My reactions are slow, so I can't always reciprocate your kindness, but please know it lingers in my mind for a long time after – sometimes forever. Your smile tells me you're not going to hurt me, that the world still hold kindness and that being out in it is not as scary as it feels.

Everyone in the airport is twice as tall as I am in my seated frame. My aunt pauses just above a large screen which displays all the airport's flight details.

'The check-in's open,' I tell her.

'Where do you see that?' she asks, as though unable to believe that my muddled mind is able to find it before her.

'Third from the bottom,' I say, watching a large family hurry towards the check-in while juggling bags, trolleys and children.

'Ah, yes. Ok, let's head to the check-in,' she informs me, as though I have any say in where I'm going.

She pushes my chair forwards and we move like a fallen leaf in a river, the steady current of people carrying us onwards.

Aunt Beth halts before a maze of red fabric tape.

'Right,' my aunt says, sounding startled, before adding with determination, 'You take this…' She comes to the front of me and lifts the suitcase onto the chair, positioning it so that the case's weight is resting on the handles of the chair and not on me. '…If you just hold it there…are you ok like that? Can you see?'

'It's fine,' I say, wrapping my arms around the case to stop it from falling off.

Our check-in only has a few people waiting in its line, so the space is clear for us to weave our way to the end, by which time there's no one left to check in except us.

I struggle in the movement and the noise to take in what the woman behind the desks is saying, but my aunt has it all under control as she hands various bits of paper and our passports to the woman. A label is attached to my chair and we're instructed to go to the wheelchair assistance area. When we get to our instructed area, I watch the people about us as my aunt speaks to the person in charge of the wheelchair assistance. The flight's only an hour and a half. We're not even leaving the country but somehow it feels as though we are: perhaps it's all the excited and harassed people bustling about us that make it feel that way.

Suddenly, I'm grabbed from behind and pushed forwards. I grab onto the arms of the chair, my stomach leaping into my chest so hard that I'm sure it will leave a bruise. I try desperately to look around but I'm too stiff and the chair's too constraining. I know it's not my aunt who's grabbed me: I can smell male deodorant and my aunt wouldn't grab me in that way. I try to speak loudly over all the noise but the person doesn't seem to hear or just doesn't care enough to stop and listen. I have no idea where we're going or what's going to happen next. Then my aunt appears alongside us, her legs moving quickly to catch up with the guy who's apparently left her behind. As we move through the airport it gets busier and busier, but still the guy doesn't slow. I think he thinks it's fun to use me and my chair as a human barricade to get through the crowds, as people leap out of the way when they see us coming, jumping forwards or backwards with their bags and jackets swiping dangerously close to my face. I lurch forwards, pain shooting along my hips and shoulders as he abruptly stops to avoid a large family – who can't get out of the way in time.

We're taken into a lift and taken upwards; a moment later we stop and I hear doors open but the doors in front of me don't move. Instead, I'm dragged backwards. I desperately want him to stop. I don't like this. I want my aunt to tell him to stop what he's doing but she's just walking quickly beside us. There are not even any brakes on this stupid chair that I could pull to make him stop. We get through security quite quickly and a kind-faced lady gives me such a thorough frisking in my chair that it leaves me slightly perturbed. Again I'm pushed face first through the crowd until we come to an area tucked away from everyone else. The man lets go of the handles and I roll forwards a little.

'Someone will come and get you and take you to the plane,' he says, sounding bored.

He seems utterly unaware that he has literally been in control of my life for the last ten minutes. He has chosen where I walk, how fast I move, where I stop and now, as I stare at the scuffed cream wall I've been dumped in front of (when I could have been placed before the wide window which shows all the planes or facing something…anything, other than this expanse of wall), I realise he had control over what I see, too.

My aunt turns me round so that I can see both out of the window and to the crowd beyond our quiet corner. Perhaps some people would be offended, being tucked away, out of sight and out of mind, but I'm glad for this quieter space, away from the bustle and the looks people give me when I'm in this chair.

Aunt Beth sits beside me in one of the chairs which line the wall.

'Your grandad would be glad to see this getting some use,' Aunt Beth remarks, looking at the wheelchair.

'Mhh,' I sound disgruntledly.

'I keep thinking about getting rid of it, but it comes in handy every now and then.'

'Yeah,' I mutter irritably.

I know she's trying to distract me by talking to me, but I really wish she'd stop. So much of me hurts from being in this stupid chair that everything she says annoys me and I don't want to snap at her.

I'm glad when we're joined by a few elderly people in wheelchairs while we wait because my aunt chats away to them while I get to sit mostly in silence.

'Hello,' says a cheery man in his early fifties coming to the front of my chair. His uniform informs me he works here. 'My name's Allan. How are you?'

'Fine, thanks, yourself?' I say, a little startled by the contrast in the assistance workers.

'I'm very good, thank you,' he says brightly. Doing up his hi-vis jacket. 'I'm going to take you down to the plane. Do you have your passes?'

Aunt Beth hands them to him and he checks them over before giving them back.

'Have you got everything you need?' he asks, looking around the chair for any dropped or forgotten bags.

'I think so,' my aunt says, sounding more relaxed than she has done all day.

'Ok, we're going to go through those double doors and along the corridor,' he tells me, moving to the back of my chair.

Allan keeps a running commentary as we move through the

airport, his pace steady and in keeping with my aunt's. Each time we stop he explains why, and when we go on the lift he tells me before he rolls me backwards. We go outside and even there he prepares me for the bumps in the tarmac. Allan explains what will happen as I'm taken onto an ambulift – which looks like a cross between a lift and a crane. Then I'm wheeled onto the aircraft.

My hands grip tightly onto the arms of the chair as my heart lurches at the sight of all the people on the plane. The air hostess tells me where my seat is and I heave myself out of the chair so that it can be taken away because it's too wide to be wheeled down the aisle. I wish they'd checked the passes before telling me to get up because now I'm left clinging to the back of someone's seat and Aunt Beth's arms are too full of bags, jackets and boarding passes to help me. I begin to move down the aisle, pausing and waiting repeatedly for people to put their stuff in the overhead lockers and move out of the way so I can get past. I grab at the back of each seat to help me walk, my legs feeling like they might give out from under me.

I slowly look behind me to see that Aunt Beth is stuck three rows behind me. When I turn back around I see that most of the passengers are staring at me, examining my slow progression like I'm the pre-flight entertainment. I can tell by the looks on many of their faces that they're trying to figure out what's wrong with me, while others watch with pity…I'm a human being, not an exhibition to be objectified and gawked at; I don't want your pity…I just hoped for your respect, I want to yell, but of course I don't – that would be rude.

'Our seats are the next one,' my aunt says, having caught up to me.

My spine and hips crack with the disjointed angle I have to

put them into to squeeze down our row of seats before I sink gratefully into my window seat. I could have sat in the middle, but I don't want to sit next to a stranger or at the aisle where people will be walking past me and reaching over me to get to their belongings from the overhead lockers.

'I thought they let sick people on first,' I whisper to Aunt Beth, glad that the chairs mostly hide me from sight.

'They used to. When I took your grandad on a plane in a wheelchair they let us on before everyone else and they let us sit in the first row. The air hostess said they've just changed the rules. When we land I'll call and get our seats moved forward for the flight back. We still won't be at the front, though – it's not allowed,' she explained, picking through the reading material on the back of the chair in front of her. 'Do you want a magazine?'

Chapter Twenty

My aunt smooths down her smart suit that she's taken to wearing to my doctors' appointments.

When we arrive at the hotel we fall into the same routine we had in Northcairn: my aunt goes out and comes back with dinner, we eat and watch TV before going to sleep, and then the same thing happens the next day – with my aunt leaving my breakfast ready for me before she departs.

'You ready?' she asks, spotting me watching her.

I nod, too nervous to speak. We head out of the hotel to where the taxi waits for us. I wrap my arms around my stomach which churns and lurches in time to the movements of the taxi. The taxi stops at the door of a rundown building. The paint peeling off the sign above the door tells us we're at the Redress Clinic.

My aunt and I exchange dubious looks before we leave the taxi and head into the reception area. It's empty except for a couple of men and a woman behind a long desk.

'Hi, can I help you?' one of them asks with a friendly smile.

'We have an appointment with Doctor Hopefield,' Aunt Beth says in rather businesslike fashion.

'Doctor Hopefield is running a little late. Would you mind waiting in the waiting room?' she asks, pointing with her pen to the door to the right of us. 'There's a little kitchen in the dining room if you'd like to make something to drink.'

We head to the waiting room which is empty except for us. We take a seat and I lean my head back against the wall until I remember the discoloured marks at Northcairn and I heave my head back up, but there are no marks on the walls here except for a few scuff marks at ankle height.

'Are you sure this is a good idea?' I ask, looking at the dated interior and chipped floor tiles. I'm not sure what I expected... perhaps something ridiculously modern and plush like the fashionably private hospitals I see on TV.

'Of course I am...it's all going to be fine,' she tells me, but she doesn't look convinced.

'Joyce Jack?' a nurse asks, coming into the room by another door.

My aunt helps me to my feet and we follow the nurse into a wide vestibule with corridors dividing off from it. The nurse walks slowly beside us past various doors. I glance into a couple of rooms which contain hospital beds and another full of black chairs with patients occupying them. We're led into the doctor's room which looks as dated as the rest of the place. Most of one wall is covered by a book case teeming with heavy-looking books and plastic medical sculptures of bodyparts. The nurse takes a seat by the door after shutting it behind us.

'Joyce Jack,' Doctor Hopefield states, getting to her feet. She's in her mid-fifties, wearing a smart dress and suit jacket which don't quite go together. Her brown hair has been put hastily into a pearl clip. She has a slightly eccentric air to her that reminds me of a nursery teacher Sarah once had, whose voice was just as soft and commanding.

She holds out her hand for my aunt and me to shake.

'This is Doctor Khan, he's come from India to learn some of our methods. Is it ok for him to sit in on our meeting? He can wait outside if you'd rather,' she says and for some reason I have no doubt that she would send him from the room without a moment's hesitation or reluctance if I ask.

'It's fine,' I say quietly, as my aunt and I take a seat in front of Doctor Hopefield's desk.

'You're concerned about whether or not Joyce has Lyme disease,' Doctor Hopefield states, opening the file in front of her.

'Yes, I sent a letter about a week ago to explain why,' my aunt says, sounding nervous, her handbag clutched tightly in her hands.

'Yes,' Doctor Hopefield says enthusiastically, 'it was very informative. Did your GP write it for you?'

'No, I did,' Aunt Beth says, sounding slightly taken aback.

'It was very useful,' the doctor adds with a brief smile, before her attention returns to my file.

We go through the usual line of questions: when the symptoms started, how they progressed, the other diagnoses… until finally, we catch up with where I am now. I struggle to keep up with Doctor Hopefield's thoughts: she makes leaps and insights, asks questions and connects them to other things I'd said previously. She didn't make any notes, she didn't need to, everything's held in her head. From the corner of my eye I can see Doctor Khan watching her in complete wonderment. Often he, too, looks baffled by her quiet prowess – then she'll say something and you can see him suddenly making the connection she had made long before him. Never before had I been in the presence of a genius, an unrivalled master of her craft, and it's utterly fascinating to behold.

'Can you tell me what you're able to do at the moment, Joyce, in your day-to-day life?'

I have to think for a while before I can remember what I tend to do each day.

'I read a lot...erm, I do the dishes and I make dinner most nights,' I say.

I can feel myself sinking in my seat because when I'm at home it feels like these activities are huge things but saying them here, out loud...it highlights the opposite.

'Good. And do you make these meals from scratch or are they ready-made?'

'The first one,' I reply, knowing that's the right answer but unable to remember what she said.

'Can you tell me what the first one was?'

'No,' I say, swallowing hard against the lump in my throat.

'Do you have an appointment with the nutritionist today?' Doctor Hopefield asks.

'Yes, we do,' Aunt Beth replies when I look to her for the answer.

'Good. Whether Joyce has Lyme or ME it will be useful to you to see him. Would it be all right if Clair takes your measurements?' Doctor Hopefield asks me.

I nod and get heavily to my feet. I follow Clair, the nurse, to the back of the room where she takes my weight, height and temperature before asking me to sit on the edge of the bed as she pulls out a step for me to climb up. She then takes my blood pressure and pulse.

'Pulse is 179,' the nurse says calmly, but there's an edge of unease in her voice which makes me look to Doctor Hopefield.

'Can you take it again?' the doctor asks, breaking off her

conversation with my aunt.

'I've taken it twice,' the nurse replies.

Doctor Hopefield stands up and comes over to us. She takes my wrist and feels for herself.

'It is very fast,' she says thoughtfully. 'Are you feeling nervous?'

'No, not really,' I say honestly, my anxiety from earlier long faded.

'We'll take it again before you leave,' the doctor recommends. 'Your hands are very cold. Do you find they turn blue at times?'

I nod before adding, 'My feet are the same.'

'Yes, poor circulation…brain response? Yes,' Doctor Hopefield says to herself. 'Come and feel her pulse, Dr Khan,' Doctor Hopefield orders, before quickly adding to me in a softer tone, 'Only if that is all right for him to feel?'

I nod and let Dr Khan take my wrist.

'I'm going to check your reflexes,' Doctor Hopefield says when Dr Khan's finished. 'Watch, closely, Mr Khan. Clair, are you ready to write this in the notes for later?'

With Clair's clipboard and pen at hand, Doctor Hopefield begins. She takes a metal wand which looks like it has a plastic shark's tooth at the end of it from a tray of instruments; she knocks it against my knees and elbows – making them jump like some of my more aggressive twitches. She asks me to lie back on the bed before she examines my stomach and asks me questions about my bowel movements. She then takes from her tray a metal, two-pronged instrument with a flat metal disk at the other end.

'Can you hear this?' she asks, pinging the prongs and quickly holding them to my ear.

Unprepared, I flinch strongly as the noise sharply reverberates inside my ear and radiates to my brain. She pats my arm in apology.

'Can you feel this?' she says, pinging the prongs again, but this time holding the flat end to various parts of my body.

'Yes,' I say repeatedly, as the vibrations go into my tissue.

Doctor Hopefield then lifts my leg and places one hand under the joint while using her other hand to flex my leg; then she checks my other joints and examines my feet and neck; asking me questions as she goes about the pain and symptoms I get in the various parts of me that she examines. My ears, eyes and mouth are even checked…I'm literally examined from the inside out. I'm more than used to being examined but never – in all my years of illness – have I had all of me examined in one go.

'Yes…' she mutters wistfully, more to herself than to me. She pats my hand kindly before stating factually, 'You're very weak.'

'If you wouldn't mind standing here for me,' she instructs, pointing to the spot just in front of her.

Clair gives me a hand down from the bed and leaves me to stand on my designated spot.

'If you can, could you stand with your feet together and then close your eyes and go up onto your toes for me?' she asks.

I do as she asks, closing my eyes and pushing myself up onto my toes – hands from all directions grab me to stop me from falling as I wobble precariously, the heels of my feet barely an inch off the ground.

'Ok, let's leave that, shall we?' Doctor Hopefield says, sounding slightly crestfallen. 'Take a seat,' she says to me, sitting in her seat behind the desk and closing over my file.

'The timeline you've given of Joyce's health, where she had a summer cold and then started noticing some rather severe symptoms about six months later, coupled with her list of symptoms that I have from your letter and the results from my examination, leave me confident in clinically diagnosing you with Lyme disease. With your permission, I would like to send some blood off to the laboratories to see if we can get a positive Lyme test. If we can get a positive test, then the results will help me determine if you have any coinfections and what treatment we should put you on.'

'How long will it take to get better?' I ask desperately.

'It's hard to say when I haven't seen any blood work, but other patients with similar physical and neurological severity tend to take about five years to start making any improvements,' she says, a pained look momentarily escaping her professional mask of concealment as my aunt whispers…

'Five years.'

I stare numbly at an ornament of three little elephants on Doctor Hopefield's desk, each elephant connected to the other by their trunk that wraps around the elephant in front of its tail as they march – suspended in time.

'I can't promise that you'll ever be able to do the things you once did or that you can ever return to school, college or be able to work…but I can promise to give you a fighting chance,' she says consolingly.

Then what's the point? I think to myself. Caged…well enough to peek at the world but never well enough to join it, able to do and live life's small things but never able to do something worth living for. I picture myself in my forties, standing at the same kitchen sink, washing the same dishes, my elderly aunt putting me to bed when I'm too ill to stand alone…I've condemned us both. I grip the outsides of my thighs, my nails digging into my skin as I well with emotion, my eyes threatening to spill the tears I'm fighting to hold back. I scold myself for it, this isn't me, I don't cry...stupid disease, stupid me.

When the appointment ends, my aunt and I are taken to the ward full of black chairs, where Nurse Clair leaves us to wait for the nurse who will take my blood.

'These are nice,' my aunt says, sitting in one of the plush black chairs.

'Yeah,' I reply with disinterest.

'Look, they recline and they have footstools,' she says looking around the room at the other patients and the way they've placed their chairs. 'I hate to think how much they cost.'

'Hi, Joyce Jack?' another nurse asks, coming over to us with what looks like a miniature milk crate with phials instead of bottles.

I nod in confirmation.

'Are all those for me?' I ask, looking at all the phials.

'I'm afraid so,' the nurse says, putting a pillow under my arm and tying a tourniquet above my elbow.

'These are nice chairs,' my aunt comments.

'Thanks,' the nurse says with a toothy smile. 'They're slowly upgrading the place. The patients' equipment is done first – it's important people are comfortable when they're here all day.'

'I've never seen a needle like that before,' I remark, looking at the thin needle she's placing in my arm; I'm so used to needles I barely acknowledge the sharpness as it goes in.

'It's a butterfly needle. They're more expensive so public hospitals don't tend to use them, but it's better for your veins, especially if you've had a lot of blood taken from them in the past.'

Aunt Beth nods: clearly all her doubts about this place have been eradicated. I watch as the thirteenth phial is changed for a new one and as the red blood goes squirting into it.

'Oh my...' Aunt Beth sounds, with a disgusted look on her face.

'You're not scared of blood,' I point out.

'No, it's just when it bounced off the bottom.' She shudders and the nurse and I exchange an amused look.

I watch the other patients, many of whom are chatting to one another, utterly at ease with each other and the potions dripping from tubes into many of their arms or the blood being drawn from their veins. This is a world where the sick dominate the healthy and where the healthy accept the sick. The way the nurses and doctors join in and chat with the patients makes it feel more like a gathering of old friends. This is a safe place to be sick, I realise: you don't have to be guarded here or try to persuade people that you're ill...because they already believe you.

Chapter Twenty-One

In the time between our hospital visit and the results coming in, I turned nineteen. It's safe to say I was far from celebrating the reminder that yet another year had been lost to me and that I had nothing to show for it or the past two birthdays which had come before it. I wanted to ignore it entirely, but I was grateful nonetheless for the effort my aunt went to to get me a surprise cake from my favourite bakery.

It took six weeks for the blood results to come in and I was surprised when I opened the thick envelope, addressed to my aunt and me, to find the actual lab results. When I phone the GP or the hospital for my results, I'm simply told if they came back as being positive or negative, I'm not allowed to actually see what's going on inside me.

Aunt Beth told me that the private hospital sends the blood to America and Germany and that's why it takes six weeks for the results; it's also how the private hospitals are able to get different results from the public hospitals. Why the discrepancy? Well, the cynical would say it's to hide the true number of people with the disease; other cynics would say that it's a great way to keep the already overstretched budget down, while others would question whether to misdiagnose and label as crazy is easier than trying to treat someone with a near impossible disease to cure.

I don't understand any of the sequenced numbers and letters but I do understand the graphs, where the normal is in red and the patient is in blue. I understand that when the blue exceeds the red it's a positive result – almost all of mine are over the red, some by nearly double. Aunt Beth won't confirm what I suspect the results mean, even though she's become something of an expert; her bedside table is stacked high with books and research notes on Lyme disease.

I gaze at the sheets of paper as my aunt lays them out on the kitchen table before me. It's ten in the morning, the equivalent of midnight to the chronically ill, but it was the only appointment Aunt Beth could get this week and she was eager to find out what the doctor would say. It's been interesting over the past few weeks because I've been finding out more and more about what happened in my appointments with the doctor and nutritionist, as Aunt Beth goes over it on the phone with Sarah and Kate: I hadn't remembered half of what had been said or done and what had seemed like twenty-minute appointments had actually been well over the separate two hours we'd paid for.

'I thought you'd sent that?' I say, looking at the questionnaire I was asked to fill out and post back to the private hospital.

'I did but I made a copy for my files,' Aunt Beth says, pointing to the folder at the end of the table.

How did we come to this? I wonder, that my old history folder which has a drawing of a knight riding an old nag and a Viking in a Victorian lady's dress on the front of it – drawn by Connor one bored afternoon in school – has now become my medical file.

When I compare our list of symptoms to the one provided by the private hospital's questionnaire…it's safe to say we missed more than a few but I'd grown so used to most of them that I forgot they were symptoms and not normal to feel.

The full list of symptoms for those with Lyme contains:

- Sweats
- Chills
- Fevers
- Flushing
- Fatigue/exhaustion/poor stamina
- Swollen glands
- Sore throat
- Pelvic pain
- Testicular pain
- Menstrual irregularity
- Bladder irritability
- Breast pain
- Nausea
- Constipation
- Diarrhoea
- Rib sourness
- Chest pain
- Shortness of breath
- Cough
- Heart palpitations
- Neck/back stiffness
- Neck pain
- Joint pain
- Joint swelling
- Joint stiffness
- Muscle pain
- Muscle cramps

- Twitching muscles
- Numbness/tingling
- Facial paralysis
- Blurred vision
- Floaters
- Light sensitivity
- Ear buzzing/ringing
- Ear pain
- Sound sensitivity
- Hair loss
- Poor balance
- Headaches
- Fainting
- Tremor
- Confusion
- Difficulty thinking
- Forgetfulness
- Difficulty speaking
- Word-finding difficulty
- Difficulty writing
- Reversing numbers/letters
- Depression/anxiety
- Mood swings
- Disturbed sleep
- Disorientation/getting lost/going to wrong place.

I pick up the pen and start doodling on the notepad Aunt Beth left for me to take notes with, hoping that the distraction will calm my nerves. Oddly enough, it's not the results which worry me –

it's having to speak on the phone. Until the other day, when the appointment was confirmed, I hadn't realised how much I'd been avoiding speaking on the phone. I try to remember the last time I did…eight months…over a year? It's hard to say but I remember the difficulty of it all too clearly: without the person speaking before me I couldn't follow the cue for when I was to speak; the person on the end of the phone (a salesperson, I think) became belligerent and impatient with me for not replying, their words got jumbled and in my panic I struggled to speak coherently, and each time the subject changed unexpectedly I was left baffled as my brain tried to catch up.

My aunt double-checks everything on the table as I draw a swirling hurricane. Dog's lying quietly in his basket, watching our every move as though he can sense our anticipation.

'I wish it had a loudspeaker,' Aunt Beth remarks, looking at the phone as though it has done her a great disservice.

She was close to frantic last night when she jabbed at every button on the phone, trying to make it perform a function it wasn't ever designed to do. I found it galling that she was so desperate to listen in and be a part of the conversation, to the point that she even planned to go out early this morning and buy a new phone; luckily, she slept in. I suppose she is paying for it and from her point of view, I forget everything, so what's the point of the doctor speaking to just me? But still…it's my body and I feel as though nothing about it is private anymore. My family openly discuss it, the doctors freely probe it, and I have no choice but to honestly answer their most intimate of questions.

Automatically, Aunt Beth snatches the phone from the table as its ring fills the kitchen, clutching it in her hand for a couple of rings and then handing it to me. I wonder if she was considering answering it or whether she just didn't want the doctor to know that we've been waiting with notepads and pens at the ready.

'…Hello,' I say.

'Hello, is that Joyce Jack?' Doctor Hopefield's distinctive voice comes through the phone.

'Ehm – yes.'

'It's Doctor Hopefield. How are you?' she asks.

'I'm fine, thanks, how are you?' I ask back, my breath catching in my throat.

'Oh well, I'm very well, thank you,' she answers, sounding genuinely delighted to have been asked. 'Have there been any changes in your condition recently?'

'No, not really,' I answer.

I try to avoid my aunt's gaze as she mouths, 'What's she saying?'

'Well, I have your results here. Do you have a copy in front of you? We can go through them and I'll explain what they all mean and then we can discuss treatment options.'

Doctor Hopefield goes through every page of my results. I try to take notes while I listen, which my aunt eagerly reads over my arm. At least twice she moves her chair closer to me as the call continues, and as the conversation goes on I become increasingly aware of her head slowly moving closer and closer to me and the phone by my ear. Doctor Hopefield tells me that I definitely have Lyme disease and three coinfections. (Infections ticks can carry in addition to the Lyme. It's like buy one get a selection free, each is a separate infection yet they so often come as a package.) Doctor Hopefield explains that ideally she would put me on intravenous antibiotics but that would require me to be at the private hospital. Intramuscular injections weren't an option as my aunt doesn't have the training required to administer them, which leaves pulsed antibiotics.

This tactic requires three different types of antibiotic. I would take two types of antibiotic for four days, say Monday to Thursday, and then I'd switch to take the third antibiotic for three days, Friday to Sunday. The idea, and one of the reasons that Lyme is so difficult to treat, is that when the Lyme is attacked, it starts to coat itself in a biofilm (basically a wall of steel) to protect itself. As I switch antibiotics it has to change the type of biofilm that it's covered itself with – meaning that it never gets the chance to fully protect itself from one antibiotic before a new one comes and it has to start all over again because the drug has a different make-up and therefore works differently to the one/ones that came before it, so the previous biofilm won't be effective. At this point I hand the phone over to Aunt Beth for the treatment and financial costs to be explained to her.

'Well…' my aunt says when she hangs up the phone. '… What do you think?'

'How are you going to pay for it? You have Kate to support, and Sarah. We barely manage as it is,' I point out.

'That's for me to worry about,' Aunt Beth tells me with a bright smile; her eyes lit up in a way that they haven't been for a long time. 'They really sound like they know what they're doing.'

'She's a Lyme specialist, isn't she?' I say, lacking her enthusiasm.

'Joyce, this is good. We're going to get you better. We should celebrate, I'll get a chippy…or I could get something else from the shops,' she adds when she sees my face at the idea of a fatty and greasy chippy which will only make me nauseous. 'You have a think and let me know what you fancy.'

'Ok,' I say flatly as Aunt Beth gets up from her chair and puts on her work jacket.

She kisses the top of my head before saying gently, 'Why don't you go back to bed, you must be tired.'

'Yeah,' I reply impassively.

'I'll phone your cousin and sister tonight to tell them,' she calls eagerly as she heads to the front door, leaving me alone in the darkening kitchen as the rain clouds cluster outside the window – drowning out the light.

Even with the doctor's warning, Aunt Beth seems to think this will be easy but then, she's never felt it inside of her, moving and attacking her, she's never felt the monster within or how powerful it's grown. It's not going to go quietly into the night, it's going to do the same thing as me and do everything it can to survive.

Chapter Twenty-Two

I would like to introduce myself, I feel it's only fair. Only I know you so well now, you might get a scare. I know you know I'm in there, though I crept with greatest stealth: I am the hidden monster buried within yourself.

There's no need to feel privileged, that I picked you amongst the rest. I'm glad to be of service, I give you only my very best.

I know they promised you they'd find me, but all I'll do is misdirect. I'm a hundred illnesses in one, the master of disguise. I'll leave no clues that they can find, only false crumbs, that will slowly grind them down. Eventually I'll make them crack and they'll tell you I'm all in the mind.

I know you now have a name for me and yet still I have three: Lyme, Borrelia burgdorferi and spirochaete, I don't mind which you choose. You can try and fight against me, but I'm a force of such great might, that I already make you scream at night. I exhaust you during the day and then I keep you up all night. I've poisoned your mind so that you're crippled with doubt.

I am the puppet master, the master of your world. I pick at your skin and tug on your limbs to remind you who's in charge. So just think of what I'll do to you, if you try to start a fight: I'll claw at your bones and I'll break your joints, I'll drag you through the darkness and I'll torture you so that you never see the light.

You may kill some of my soldiers but their bodies will poison your blood. Your organs may start failing while I continue my jolly jaunt. To think you could have been rid of me so easily, but now we're bound for life. I float about your blood, I tunnel through your organs, I nest inside your mind, your tissue and muscles are an added delight. From time to time I'll fade away and you'll think you've won the fight and just as you give in to hope, I'll come back to take another bite.

I sit numbly at the kitchen table for a long time, unsure of what to do. After a time, I stand up and go to the sink. Out of habit I begin filling it with warm, soapy water and start piling the dirty dishes amongst the white bubbles. I pick up the last plate from under the water and I feel something slide off it, once the plate's been wiped clean. I reach into the water for whatever fell off, gasping sharply as something pierces the side of my wrist. I pull my arm from the water to find a shard of glass embedded in my skin, deep red blood dripping from its transparent end. I grab and tear off a few sheets of kitchen paper to protect my fingers as I pull it out – gritting my teeth against the slicing pain. I drop the shard of glass onto the worktop and hasten to the utility sink, the kitchen roll wrapped around my bleeding wrist. I run the cold water over the wound, trying to clean it. Hopefully it's been bleeding so much that the dirty dishwater has been washed out with the blood. It doesn't look as deep as I thought it might be. I pause, transfixed by the blood dripping into the running water below, the diluted red blood swirling in the current which carries it down the drain.

It's in there…in my blood. I look at the blood which has dripped onto the floor, then down at myself; it's everywhere. I press hard on the skin around the wound, making it bleed. I want to squeeze it out, every last drop. I shake my head, realising how futile that is, I furiously wash the blood from my arm and then wrap the wound in fresh kitchen roll and press it tightly against the wound – uncaring of how much the pressure hurts. The moment it stops bleeding I go back to the kitchen and rummage with my good arm for antiseptic cream and a plaster. Then I methodically bleach the sink in the kitchen and utility, the spots where my blood dripped onto the stone floor and the worktop where I left the shard of glass. I stare about the kitchen, hunting feverishly for anything I might have missed, the stench of bleach stinging my noise and making my chest ache with each breath. When I finally concede that there's nothing left for me to bleach, I put the bottle away, and as I do, I find I now have a name for the sensation which has plagued me since I became unwell; it's not just that I'm ill, it's that I feel dirty, contaminated…and diseased.

I look up at the kitchen mirror to see the person who holds no resemblance to me watching me.

'Why won't you die? Why won't you die!' I scream.

The face of the person watching me crumples; its hand tries to cover its mouth as a cry escapes through its fingers. The person in the mirror disappears as my body sinks to the floor, my arms wrapped around my middle as I gasp for air – winded by the loss of myself. I feel it in my soul as the howl from my mouth fills the kitchen – so animalistic, so full of pain that it can't be contained.

I rock back and forth as the sound keeps coming, even my gasps are a raggedy cry. I feel like my soul has been ripped through my gut, the wound lined with shards of glass so every movement and every breath slices me deeper. My lips and face start to tingle from the lack of air, my world goes blurry – I don't know how long I lie there. Eventually exhaustion takes over and the dam of numbness somehow rises once more. I spot Dog watching me from under the table, his body rigid and his eyes afraid.

'I'm sorry,' I whisper and he cautiously comes to me.

We lie on the floor together until I find the strength to get up. I clasp my injured wrist and hold it to my chest as I watch the branches of the trees swaying undecidedly in all directions from the kitchen window. I slowly head outside, leaving the back door open to rid the kitchen of the stench of bleach. I sit on the garden bench, the wind blowing my scraggily auburn hair across my face. I wrap my arms around me against the cold wind but it feels so clean and pure in my lungs that I long for more and as I sit there I take deep breaths of it as though it will purify me. The dark clouds release the odd spots of rain as I sit looking out dazedly at the garden.

How am I meant to fight against something that's inside of me? That I can't see or feel before me. I can't reason with or scream at. How do I tame the most powerful kind of predator and the smartest of stalkers? I know it can kill me. I know it's killed others but it'll keep me alive so that it can live, too – that's what makes it so smart. Its resourcefulness is astounding, its intelligence unrivalled, and its determination to survive unbeaten.

This treatment feels futile. This disease has dominated and infiltrated me to the point that it is who I am. I know the treatment won't cure me. I am a sick person, that is my identity, it is all that I am. I learned how to be that person but I don't know how to get better or how to survive in the in-between. Right now, I'm in the storm but once it calms the true extent of the damage will be revealed and I don't know who I will have to become to survive it. The status of being sick gives me protection against all I have lost.

What if I'm one of the people who don't get better, despite the treatment? Am I to lose the hope of getting better as quickly as I found it? What will become of me if my last hope fails?

I watch the wind as it ripples through the long grass which is desperately needing to be cut and the hedges which need trimming. Dog strolls towards me, having followed me outside. He presses his warm body against my legs, his noise twitching to smell the scents the wind brings. The long grass tickles my ankles and at first I let it, but then the sensation makes me feel like something's crawling up my legs; I check them over but there's nothing there. I look out to the garden, my eyes following a bird as it flies into the hedge, reminding me of a programme I once watched, where they took apart an empty bird's nest and found three ticks, and of another where the hedgehog the woman was checking over for fleas had eleven ticks pulled from it. I watched the programme long before I knew about Lyme disease and the programme never even mentioned the illness. I wonder if there are still hedgehogs and mice living under the wood store or how many bird's nests there are in the hedges and the trees. I stand up and go back inside with Dog...I don't feel safe outside anymore.

I go to my room to get a jumper and come back to the kitchen a moment later with my phone. I'm sure I went through for something else though, I think to myself. I go to my room to get a jumper, the next thing I know I'm in the utility room. I look about me, unsure of why I'm here. I'm certain I was in my room. I wrap my hands around my cold arms and head to my room to get a jumper. Inside my room, I look about for the thing I came to my room for – unable to remember. I grab my jumper and put it on...I'm sure whatever I forgot will come back to me.

The school corridors were crammed with students all heading to their next class. I let the crowd carry me forwards, my next class straight ahead. My heart lurched in my chest and I pushed myself against the corridor wall, my eyes searching frantically around me. Students, their bags and folders, knocked against me as I stood like a stone jutting out from a river. I couldn't move forwards…an invisible barrier was stopping me from moving onwards. I knew where my classroom was and I could see it in my mind's eye. I'd been in this school for more than half a decade and knew it blindfolded, yet I didn't know where to go; I felt lost but I knew that wasn't possible. I pushed through the crowds to the stairs opposite me, hurrying up them and along the corridors and through three sets of doors until I reached another flight of stairs; I went down them and headed to my class from a different direction. The corridors were empty now. I didn't need the teacher's scowl to tell me I was late.

'Sorry,' I muttered as I headed to my seat next to Amy.

'Hi,' Amy said nervously.

'Are you ok?' I asked, glancing at the teacher to make sure he wasn't looking.

'Yeah…I just wasn't sure if you were speaking to me,' Amy said softly, her shoulders rounded and her eyes not meeting mine. 'I said hi to you earlier and you completely ignored me.'

'Oh, I mustn't have seen you,' I said, glancing at the page number Amy's looked up before finding it in my own book.

'Joy, you were looking right at me.'

I was walking along the upstairs corridor where all the science and computer classes are. The newer part of the building had been freshly painted and my steps were all but silent on the new carpet. I strolled along it contently, then I halted, looking about me in alarm: I was downstairs in the language and history corridor at the opposite end of the school and I'd no idea how I got here. The older building had an off-cream colour on the walls which looked grubby under the harsh lighting, the tiled floors were cream-coloured with flecks of black running through them. I looked about me, searching for clues. The sound of a nearby teacher talking to their class was the only sign of life in the deserted corridor. Why was I here? Where was I supposed to be? What class was I meant to be in? Had I gone to the bathroom or was I on an errand for a teacher? I didn't even know what day it was.

Chapter Twenty-Three

Me: Is it ok if I come to yours instead? My aunt can drop me off at the farm office. She's going past yours anyway.

Logan: Yeah, if you're sure. I can take you home after.

Me: Thanks. I'll see you tomorrow at one-ish. Before I forget again, can you tell your Uncle Davey I said thanks for telling me about Lyme? I hope Alice is doing better.

**

'Will you call me if you need picking up?' Aunt Beth insists the next day as she drives down the farm track.

'Logan said he would take me home,' I remind her.

'I know but if you get tired and you can't get away, then send me a message and I'll come and get you,' she tells me as we come to a stop outside the outbuildings.

'Thanks,' I say gratefully as I take off my seat belt.

'Ok, well, call me,' she reminds as I get out of the car before adding quickly, 'Should I walk you somewhere?'

'Ehh, I'll phone him so I know which building he's in,' I say. 'Bye.'

I shut the door before calling Logan's number: he doesn't answer but I can hear his phone ringing from inside one of the barns. I wave to Aunt Beth as I walk to the large door which stands ajar. I can see Logan inside so I wave to Aunt Beth that she can go. Ever since my stay in the public hospital she's been more cautious about leaving me anywhere before knowing that I'm either with someone she trusts or that I'm somewhere safe. Her requirements are somewhat flawed, seeing as I live alone in the house all day and that's where I left to go running from, but I understand her paranoia about my safety because I experience the same for hers.

'Hi,' I say as I slip through the gap in the barn door.

'Joy, hi. What are you doing here?' Logan says, a confused crease between his eyes.

'Em, I said I was going to come round…didn't I?' I question.

'Oh yeah, sorry I forgot,' he says distractedly, dumping bags of feed onto the back of an unhitched trailer.

'Are you ok?' I ask uncertainly, taking a couple of steps further into the barn.

'Yeah, I'm fine,' he says dully, wiping his dusty hands on his trouser legs.

'Should I go? I can get my aunt to pick me up,' I say hesitantly, wrapping my hand around my elbow while wondering if Aunt Beth's still outside.

'Erm…No, no of course not,' he says with an attempt at a smile.

'Logan, what's wrong?' I ask.

'Nothing. Just let me finish this. Here, take a seat,' he says, pointing to the hay bales which I sat on before.

I look at them, unsure of how safe they are to sit on. The thought of all those ticks in the long grass, bundled up into hay bales, makes me uneasy. Those little bloodsuckers can survive an alarmingly long time without sustenance.

'Can I sit on the quad bike?' I ask, spotting two that weren't there the last time.

'Yeah, sure.'

I sit amongst a stony silence as Logan finishes what he's doing.

'I never knew you had quad bikes,' I say to break the quietness.

'Yeah, we've had them a while. Dad's not really a fan of them, but that's because he keeps tipping his over. His one's broken but we could go up to Brier Point on mine if you want?' Logan suggests, manoeuvring his quad bike out from behind the one I'm sitting on.

'Em...' I sound reluctantly, looking at the bike I'm sitting on. 'Do they have helmets?'

'No...but I can give you my ear protectors?' he suggests, sitting astride his bike.

The Joyce in me is reminding me I'm sick and that I don't need an injury to boot, but another part of me that's still Joy doesn't care.

'Where are your ear protectors?' I say, with a small smile.

'They're on the hook over there...but I'll get them,' he adds quickly, hopping off the bike and swiftly grabbing them from the hook on the wall.

I get up and sit sideways on Logan's bike before attempting to swing my leg over the seat, but my body's so stiff nowadays it's far from easy.

'I can't straddle things the way I used to,' I say awkwardly, when I notice Logan watching me.

'Never thought I'd hear you say that,' he says, struggling to keep the smile off his face.

'I…you know what I mean,' I fluster.

He hands me the ear protectors and carefully climbs on in front of me.

'You ready?' he asks.

'Yeah – no, wait. How did you know I needed ear protectors?'

'I looked Lyme disease up when you told me you had it,' he tells me.

'Oh right,' I say, taken aback.

I put the protectors on as he starts the engine – it juts forward and I grab the back of Logan's jacket to keep me steady. We head out of the barn and along the track, cutting off into an open field and then through a forest track until we clear the trees and go back into the fields. I suspect Logan is driving far more carefully than he normally would because his speed sometimes increases before quickly slowing, as if he's reminded himself that I'm holding on at the back. The fields are relatively smooth to go over, but as we reach the dirt track which takes us up the long, sloping track of the hill, the ground becomes pitted with holes and Logan slows to carefully avoid them as best as he can.

At the top of the hill he turns off the engine and I take off my ear protectors. I'm glad he gave them to me: they didn't cut out the noise entirely but it made the sound manageable.

'It's amazing up here,' I say, looking about me in wonder.

Down in the glen ahead of us, the farmland stretches on to meet the sea which twinkles in subdued brightness behind my sunglasses. Below us in the glens on either side are houses dispersed sparingly amongst the fields and behind us in the near distance tower the mountains, whose tops are hidden amongst the clouds, their extraordinary height making our viewpoint look small.

'Yeah, we used to come up here a lot in the holidays when we were kids with my cousin Alice and–' He breaks off as though realising what he's just said. 'You want to have a wander? Or you can just stay here,' he adds, quickly changing the subject.

Logan climbs off the quad, taking care not to hit me with his foot. When he sees me heaving my leg back over the bike he holds out his hand to help steady me. We wander a short distance, the movement easing the stiffness from my hips after sitting so awkwardly, my slow pace letting Logan stride out ahead of me. When the aching eases I head back, leaving Logan to wander. I sit sideways on the bike and look out at the colours of the fields, each different depending on what's being grown inside of them. The sheep and cattle graze so leisurely that it feels like time is slow in moving.

'Hey, you ok?' Logan asks as he comes back towards me.

'I'm fine,' I reply, making myself smile to prove it. 'Are you? You seem…off somehow.'

'Nah, I'm fine. Actually, I'm leaving for uni in two weeks. My dad's doing a lot better and my brother, my older one, he's going to pitch in to help pay for extra help.'

'Oh, well that's great,' I say, my stomach sinking.

'Yeah. It will be good to get away from here,' he says, standing just in front of me.

I look out to the sea, trying not to take offence or to show my disappointment.

'That's really good,' I say, trying my best to sound enthusiastic. 'It must be exciting.'

'It is, well, so long as I don't fail my course,' he says.

'What are you studying again?' I ask.

'Oceanology,' he tells me, shifting from one foot to the

other. 'So I'll be studying the physical, geological, biological and chemical effects in the ocean.'

'Sorry, I should have remembered that. My memory's really bad these days,' I remark, a silence settling back between us. '…Did you pass on my message to your uncle?' I ask, just for something to say.

'I did,' he says shortly.

'Was I not meant to tell you what he said?' I say uncertainly.

'No, it's fine. It's just…we never knew she had Lyme,' Logan says, coming to the other side of the quad bike and sitting sideways like me. 'Alice had multiple sclerosis or…we thought she did.'

'How is she now?' I ask, straining my neck to see Logan's face.

'She killed herself, about a month before I moved back home.'

I try to swallow the lump in my throat, a chill spreading throughout my body.

'She left a note saying she "just wanted the pain to stop",' Logan says quietly, his head hung and his back hunched. 'Apparently my uncle got a private autopsy and it showed she never had MS, she had Lyme.'

I want to say something to make it better but I don't know what.

'…We used to visit her in the holidays and all she ever did was go on about her illness: it was all she ever talked about, it's like she was obsessed by it…I was glad when my uncle said she found it too tiring for us to visit anymore.' He shakes his head bitterly. 'But you never say anything,' he says, turning his head to look at me. 'That's why I never realised–.'

I open my mouth to speak but no sound comes out. I feel winded. Logan's unfinished sentence hangs heavily in the fresh air between us.

'She wasn't even as bad as you: she still went out into town and did things.'

'But that doesn't mean she wasn't in pain,' I manage to say.

'She shouldn't have done it,' Logan decrees. 'It's just selfish.'

'Maybe you're the one who's selfish,' I splutter.

'What?' Logan asks, askance.

'You were expecting her to live in pain.'

'Well, now the whole family's living in pain,' Logan retorts.

'That's not fair, y-you don't know,' I stammer, my heart hammering in my chest. I hesitate, trying to think of a way to explain. 'It's like I live in a baseline of pain and on bad days it soars and on good days it lowers, but the pain never ends, it never goes and it…it changes every day so you can never get used to it and all the joint pain and bone pain, all the headaches and exhaustion are just added on top. You feel it all the time…everything hurts, Logan, all the time…and that's just physical pain – the rest can be so much worse.'

'…I'm sorry,' Logan says quietly, his voice muffled by the harsh cry of a bird who screeches its solemn lament above us. 'She was still wrong to do it.'

'She would have been scared, Logan. I'm scared, all the time and it's exhausting,' I blurt out before I can stop myself.

I feel his arms wrap safely around me and I rest my head on his shoulder and say quietly, 'She just wanted the pain to stop.'

Chapter Twenty-Four

Boxes of medication begin to arrive over the following week. My Aunt Beth and I sit down at the weekend and work our way through them, piling them up on the kitchen table to ensure that everything is there and in the right quantities.

'Now these are the instructions from the doctor about your medication,' Aunt Beth explains, pointing to a sheet of paper on the table. 'And those ones there are from the nutritionist.'

When we met the nutritionist at the private hospital, my every food choice was scrutinised: the brand, the amount, the way in which it was cooked, but the nutritionist was kind and good-humoured which actually made the appointment kind of enjoyable. For the most part, my diet's pretty good but there were two poor areas – caffeine and sugar. I never realised how much I was depending on those two substances to get through the day until the nutritionist counted them. Now I'm reduced to two cups of tea a day, but I can substitute it with herbal tea and once I start my treatment I will be banned, completely, from sugar and yeast.

Antibiotics kill bacteria – be they good or bad – and our bodies need the good bacteria so, to try and keep the balance between good and bad, I have to ban myself from eating the things which the unhealthy bacteria feast on or suffer the consequences....thrush being one of them, and don't go thinking you lucky boys get to avoid this like you did childbirth, because you can get it, too.

Aunt Beth finds a large pad of paper which Kate used to use when she went through a phase of wanting to be an artist. Aunt Beth writes the name and amount of all the medication and supplements that I'll be taking along the top and then writes the days of the week along the side, placing it all into columns so that I can tick off what I've taken so far that day. Then Aunt Beth goes through all the sheets of instructions, trying to figure out what I'm to take when, before writing them on a fresh sheet of paper and colour-coding each medication/supplement – so that they're written in a different colour and are easy to find, as I'm taking some of the stuff up to six times a day.

I sit beside her, growing increasingly slouched in my chair as time goes on. I look at the pile of tubs on the table, all full of things which will help me get better. It feels oddly thrilling to see it all and the fact that there's so much that it takes up half of my aunt's kitchen table only adds to the feeling. I know treatment is going to be long and slow, but seeing it all here makes it feel like something momentous is occurring: it's as if I've reached some warped milestone.

'How is that? Is it clear enough for you to follow?' Aunt Beth asks, pushing the sheet of paper towards me.

I read the sheet with all the times I'll be taking pills written along it. It reads a little like this: hour before breakfast, breakfast, hour after breakfast, hour before lunch, lunch, hour before tea, tea, hour after tea, supper, hour after supper. And under each heading is a list of all the stuff I'll be taking.

'How am I going to fit it all in?' I ask in astonishment.

'I'm going to give you the before-breakfast one before I leave the house in the mornings, and after that you're just going to have to be really tight on your timing,' she says, getting to her feet and rummaging inside the cupboard. 'When your grandad was ill we put all his medication into eggcups. Erm, only we don't have enough.'

She shuts the cupboard door and looks about the kitchen as though for inspiration.

'I've got shot glasses in my room,' I tell her, getting to my feet and heading out of the kitchen.

'What do you mean you have shot glasses?' my aunt calls sharply after me.

'I'm nineteen,' I point out.

'We both know you weren't nineteen when you were drinking from them,' she calls after me, making me smile.

It feels nice to be in trouble for something as common as underage drinking.

'The nurse told me you should start two new tablets each day,' Aunt Beth explains when I come downstairs and start labelling eggcups and shot glasses. 'But if you get a sore stomach or nauseous then you should stop for a day or two, just to let your stomach adjust before adding anything new.'

'There is so much,' I say, a little overwhelmed as I look over all the eggcups and shot glasses, the sheets of instructions and tubs of medications and supplements.

'Yeah, but a lot of it's supplements and they're there to help your body recover from the antibiotics…and it's all been tailored to you and what your blood work says your body needs help with,' she says consolingly, watching me with a worried expression, while glancing impatiently as Dog whines at the back door to get out. 'You'll only be on the antibiotics for three months and then they'll review everything. I know it's a lot but three months isn't that long when you consider…everything.'

Aunt Beth puts a complaining Dog outside for the bathroom as I gather up all the paper. I'm putting all the instructions to one side, when my eyes catch sight of an invoice for over three thousand pounds; at the bottom it says it's one of three invoices.

'Oh, that's not for you,' Aunt Beth says hastily, coming into the kitchen and seeing what I'm looking at.

'How are you paying for this?' I ask.

'Joyce…' She sighs heavily, folding the invoices up as though she can't stand to look at them.

'Aunt Beth?' I say beseechingly.

'I have some money saved, I'm taking on more work, I'm looking into remortgaging. I've got it sorted.'

'But now we have a positive result can't we take it back to the other doctors?' I ask.

'They don't accept private results and even if they did, they'd give you a week of IV antibiotics and send you on your way, two if you were lucky. You're getting three months of antibiotics, Joyce, and you'll probably need more after that,' she rants. I stare at the wooden table like a scolded child, her tall frame towering over my slouched one. 'You'd get nothing to support your immune system, your brain or your liver or kidneys which is what many of those supplements are for. You wouldn't even have been tested for coinfections, never mind get treated for them or have a nutritionist there to tell you that the caffeine you're drinking is suppressing your thyroid glands or anything like that.'

'Ok,' I say meekly.

'I'm sorry,' Aunt Beth says, sounding deflated and suddenly tired. Rubbing her forehead with her free hand she adds, 'It just makes me a bit mad.'

'A bit?' I state.

A loud noise, somewhere between a strangled sob and a laugh, escapes my aunt. She hastily covers her mouth with her free hand as the sound fills the kitchen. I watch, utterly taken aback as her shoulders start shaking, her eyes not meeting mine.

'I'm sorry,' she says again, wiping a tear from her eye. She finally meets my gaze and bursts out laughing like a child with giggles which can't be contained.

I bite my lip as I feel something bubbling up inside of me. I try to pull the smile from my face because it's really not funny but it's all so ridiculous that it can't be anything else. Aunt Beth's holding onto a stitch in her side as I laugh with her. Both of us in a fit of hysteria, amidst the chaos of medication charts, boxes of drugs and invoices for thousands of pounds.

Chapter Twenty-Five

Logan.

Five things most healthy people experience around sick people:

- Being near you unnerves us – for most of us, illness is not a world we know much about, and the responsibility of having to do something if you're taken unwell is terrifying because we don't have a clue what to do.

- We don't always know what to say – because we don't understand the world you live in and we don't know what's ok to say or if what we say will hurt you.

- If you find your illness confusing – then we're utterly baffled.

- We just want you to be you again – sometimes our desperation/denial makes us forget you're not.

- We try our best – I know it's tempting because it must be hard to be around us, but we haven't given up on you, so don't give up on us.

'I have your shoe,' I tell Joy, as I follow her slowly to the cottage's kitchen.

'My shoe?' she says, sounding perplexed, turning on the light in the kitchen to stave off the darkness – from the rain clouds that make it feel more like winter.

'Yeah, from when...ehh, here,' I say, handing the plastic bag to her instead of explaining because I don't really want to mention her stint in hospital.

Joy opens the bag and peers inside.

'Oh, right. Thanks,' she says awkwardly, shutting the bag and dumping it in the utility room. 'Why did you have it?'

'Ehm, well, I found you...that night,' I say, sitting at the kitchen table.

'You did,' she says with surprise, sitting opposite me, and I notice how gently she sits herself down.

'Yeah. Your aunt phoned me that night to ask if you were with me. She said she couldn't find you so I said I'd drive around to see if I could spot you,' I tell Joy, as she pulls her feet onto the chair and wraps her arms around her knees. 'I tried to phone your aunt to tell her I couldn't find you, but she wasn't answering so I headed to your house and that's when I found you...well, actually I drove past you and went to your house but there was no one there. I didn't really think much of a shoe lying in the road but...I don't know, I thought I might as well go back and have a look around and there you were – face planted in a ditch and not for the first time, I might add.'

'Shut up,' she says jovially, a smile spreading across her face and breaking the tension of my words. 'You've fallen in a ditch or two.'

'That doesn't count, they were so overgrown you couldn't tell they were there,' I retort quickly, the smile on her face making me laugh. 'What is it with ditches? It's like a rite of passage around here – you have to fall into one at least once.'

'I think it's more because they line the roads that drunken teenagers walk along to get home,' she says, before adding eagerly,

'Who was it we pushed into a ditch?'

'Amy,' I remind her. 'She was gloating that she'd never fall in one so we pushed her in…Did your aunt not tell you about that night?' I ask curiously.

'No,' she says, her elation deflating slightly. 'But then I never asked. You want a cup of tea?'

'Yeah why not,' I say. 'What's this?' I ask, pulling a large chart on the table towards me to look at in more detail.

'It's for my tablets,' Joy says, getting to her feet and putting on the kettle.

'There are heaps of them,' I say in astonishment, quickly reading it over and silently trying to pronounce some of the names.

'There's another sheet and a half,' Joy tells me, adding a splash of milk to the cup.

I push the chart back across the table and put my hands on my knees, gasping and yanking my hand back as something cold and wet touches my fingers. I look under the table and put my hand on my chest.

'Your dog just tried to kill me!' I tell Joy breathlessly, trying to cover my fright, but Joy just laughs as Dog's tail drums on the floor by my feet.

I hesitate to get up as I notice Joy grab the kettle's handle with both hands, her upper body tensed under the effort – perhaps I should have made it, I ponder. Once our drinks are ready, I get up and take the cups to the table.

'Oh, thanks,' Joy says, sounding genuinely surprised.

It's strange: now I'm looking, I'm seeing things I never noticed before. She's good at hiding her illness and she's not doing anything differently to what she's done before, but now I'm seeing small things which are giving her illness away: from her slow pace, to the kettle, to the way her hand is always reaching for something to help support her, even the way she bends down to get something out of the cupboard with one hand on the worktop to help pull her back upright.

'What?' Joy says self-consciously, putting a packet of chocolate biscuits on the table.

'Nothing,' I say quickly, trying to pull the grin off my face. I feel like a secret spy who's finally cracked the code.

She pushes the packet towards me and I take a biscuit.

'You can have two,' she says with a knowing look.

'You not having any?' I ask, reaching for another.

'I'm cutting back,' she tells me.

'You do not need to lose weight,' I say incredulously.

'I'm not trying to,' she retorts defensively. 'I'm not allowed to eat sugar or yeast when I'm on my treatment, so I'm cutting back. I don't want to go cold turkey.'

'Ah sorry. So what can you eat? There's sugar in everything nowadays,' I say, taking a bite of my chocolate-covered biscuit.

'….Rice cakes,' Joy says, after a moment's consideration.

'For how long?' I ask.

'Technically three months but probably longer,' she tells me. 'Stop laughing! They've even got my fruit and caffeine intake restricted.'

'Ha, I'm sorry – it was just the look on your face when you said it. Is that why you're drinking that?' I ask, pulling a face at the purple liquid in her cup.

'It's herbal tea and it's delicious,' she tells me, with an ill-hidden look of disgust on her face as she takes a sip.

'Yeah, it looks it,' I retort with amusement. I haven't seen her this mentally aware in a while: it feels nice, her being so present.

'You packed for uni?' Joy asks, as I finish my second biscuit.

'Pretty much. It feels weird leaving for uni at the same time as my little brother,' I tell her, glancing at the rain bouncing off the window. 'It turns out I had to cut my travelling short because my dad lent my elder brother money – so when my dad hurt his back – that's why we couldn't afford to pay someone to look after the farm…he's paid my dad back now, though, and my dad's doing a lot better.'

'So you're free to go,' Joy says with a smile, but there's a hint of sadness in her voice.

'I'll be back in October and Christmas,' I remind her.

'I'm not sure I'll get to see you in October,' Joy says resignedly.

'Why?' I ask before taking a gulp of tea.

'I'll still be on treatment. I don't know how I'll be,' Joy tells me with a heavy sigh, stretching her back momentarily before it slumps back down.

'Ok, well, we can wait and see what happens. I should probably go, though,' I say. Though I'd rather stay I'm aware of how tired she's beginning to sound and how she's getting shorter and shorter in her chair as her back hunches.

I get up and head down the hall with Joy following behind me. When I open the front door it's to find the rain bouncing energetically off the stone path. I turn around and wrap my arms around Joy, hugging her tightly to me, her arms around my back and her head on my shoulder. Reluctantly, I let go and turn to leave.

'Logan,' Joy says, calling me back. 'Come here.'

I laugh as she steps toward me and gives me another quick hug.

'Please don't go ditch diving while I'm gone,' I call as I head to my car, her laugh barely audible over the rain.

Chapter Twenty-Six

I sigh heavily as I close my book and put it on the kitchen table. Now that it's cooled, I take my spoon and begin to eat my sugar-free and, as a result, rather unappetising porridge. Once I've eaten half, I pause to empty my breakfast tablets onto the table. I line them up side by side, the supplements at one end and the medications at the other, and then I add the first two of my antibiotics for today. I examine the mix of tablets and capsules, all different shapes, sizes, colours and textures, standing proudly in alignment like soldiers, my own little army, except for those at the end. The two antibiotics keep drawing my eye with sinister appeal. I scoop up the first four tablets and swallow them with a gulp of water, then quickly grab the next four and swallow them, too…until there's only the antibiotics left. I hold them in my hand; they look innocent enough, there are no spikes or rough edges, nothing to imply the sense of foreboding I feel. I swallow them before I can talk myself out of doing so. I eat the rest of my porridge, sandwiching the tablets between my breakfast, to help protect my stomach.

I glance at the clock on the wall which tells me it's half-twelve. Logan will have definitely left by now: he told me he was planning on leaving early this morning. The knowledge that he's gone leaves me feeling strangely adrift. I know I didn't see him all that much…not like when we were in school, but he was here and it was reassuring to have someone nearby. For the first time in nearly three years I felt like I had a real friend, someone who came over with a new regularity that I've not had in a long time; who would talk about anything and everything, who I'd go out with and do things with. It was normal and to me it was priceless because when you become ill, people don't come over just to catch up and muck about, they come to "visit" because that's what you do when someone's sick, but it never felt that way with Logan. Somehow, he took me with him in his tales and adventures, he made me feel a part of them rather than just a listener to his news. Logan was a tonic far stronger than any medication and a part of me hates that I miss him already because without him, the might of my aloneness bears down upon me. I never felt sad when he left after coming over; it was never bittersweet because his brightness stayed with me.

'I've still got you,' I whisper to Dog who's watching me with wide eyes from his bed in the corner, his tail thumping once or twice against its rim as though in confirmation.

I read some more of my book at the kitchen table, my stomach growing into a mixture of pain and nausea. After a while I give up, my concentration ebbing. I lift my glass to take a drink and rid my mouth of the horrible taste within it, but as I lift the glass to my lips I clatter the glass sharply against my teeth. I pull my hand away and run my tongue along my teeth. That's when I notice the water quivering in the glass from my trembling hand. I take a slow breath as my stomach churns, then hasten to the sink as my stomach heaves, trying to expel the tablets within me. I grip onto the edge of the worktop, battling to keep the tablets inside me as I feel them rising in the back of my throat. Slowly, the feeling passes and I head carefully to my dining room, my stomach tender to every move. The signs of weakness are setting in with frightening speed. I sit on the edge of my sofa bed with my head pressed low, the room hazy with dizziness. When I'm able to I sit back up, I look at the clock by my bed to discover it's only been half an hour since I took the tablets.

'It's too early,' I whisper mournfully to Dog, who's followed me through to my dining room.

I thought I'd have days before I'd feel any effects from the treatment. After a few hours the painful nausea fades and the weakness eases just in time for the next set of drugs which ignite the pain once more.

Over the next two weeks, that routine never changes but my deterioration does. I become increasingly bedbound as my strength wanes. The only time I leave my sofa bed is to go to the bathroom. Aunt Beth has taken to leaving me a flask by my bed before she leaves for work, with my allotted two cups of tea inside it, along with a thermal soup cup containing my porridge and a cool bag with a container of salad for my lunch – to ensure that I'm eating and drinking.

Aunt Beth comes home early each night to cook me my dinner. She comes through with it on a tray which has a beanbag underside. Then she sits on the edge of my bed and spoon-feeds me my dinner because she realised the reason I wasn't eating was because by the time evening came, I was too weak to feed myself. My hand can manage the journey from the plate to my mouth once or twice before my arm starts trembling with such severity that I can't keep what's on my fork from falling all over the bed. I try my best to eat everything she gives me, but my jaw hurts with the effort of chewing, it burns with fatigue and aches for hours after. Between dinner and supper my aunt brings me my ration of fruit for the day and then, for supper, she brings me a cup of milk infused with cinnamon and holds the cup for me while I drink from a straw. I wish I could say it's humiliating, that it embarrasses me to my core…I'm sure that will come with future reflection but the truth is, for now, I just don't care.

After that my aunt helps me to the bathroom, where there's a chair for me to sit on because I can't stand for the length of time it takes to brush my teeth. I rest my arms on the sink as I use the electric toothbrush which was recommended by my dentist. It's ironic, really, that my dentist, who I've had little discussion about my health with, had far more of an understanding than any of my doctors – excluding the private one. He told me to get an electric toothbrush in case I was too unwell to brush them manually – that it would do the same job but with far less effort – and he prescribed me a toothpaste to help protect my teeth against the antibiotics. From there I go to bed and lie awake until the early morning, with only my pain for company, before sleep endeavours to free me.

After a month, I wish I could say things get better, but they don't. Every time the nausea ends it reappears with the next round of antibiotics which are so potent that they make my stomach feel like it's exploded. The shock waves spread throughout my body with such force I can accurately predict when the putrid taste of them will seep up from my stomach and through my gums, making my teeth ache as the antibiotics surge up through my mouth and face like a tidal wave into my brain. The doses are so strong I can smell the medication in my urine.

It's a staggering feeling, to literally feel your mental functions die. I struggle to understand and follow what's happening on TV. I muddle and confuse my own simplistic thoughts. My memory's so poor that I don't dare take painkillers in case I forget and take more than I should; I can't even write down if I've taken any because I forget I've done it or where I've put the note to remind me. Every day is a toxic day and every day the pain gets worse as the sand smothers my insides. My fingers and toes turn purple and blue with poor circulation, my shoulders blaze with stiffness, my head never stops aching, every position I'm in is uncomfortable. And despite my efforts to eat, I'm losing weight. My hair starts falling out, not in the dramatic way you see with some treatments, it's just strands that fall all the time – habitually covering my clothes and pillows. Often a stranger will come into my room and sit on my bed, she'll put a straw into my mouth and wait patiently for me to drink from the cup she holds. The stranger looks pained sometimes, she'll hold my hand as though afraid to do anything more to console me – unsure if her movement will cause more pain than comfort. Sometimes it's not until the stranger leaves that I recognise she's my Aunt Beth.

Aunt Beth explained before I started the treatment that as the Lyme bacteria dies, it releases large amounts of toxins into my blood and tissue – which my body has to flush out. Only the toxins come so quickly and become so numerous that my body will struggle to get rid of them. This, ladies and gentlemen, is the Herx reaction. Many of the supplements I'm taking are to help reduce this and to help my liver and kidneys to function, but nothing can stop its onslaught.

In many ways I wish there was a nurse to administer my drugs for me because making myself take the very things which are hurting me, several times a day, feels tantamount to self-harm.

After two months Aunt Beth starts asking me if I want to stop, that a lot of people don't finish the treatment because they can't take the pain – so it's ok for me to stop, too. I feel like my body is shutting down. I find myself crying a lot. Silent tears fall, often unnoticed, from my eyes; I don't know why, I don't feel sad, I don't feel anything except pain. Every symptom I've ever felt has been exacerbated to a level I never knew imaginable, and upon my last month of treatment, Aunt Beth's question turns into a beseeching request but I won't stop – I can't. Swathes of time pass, my mind grows further from my body, I feel the pain but somehow my mind's disconnected me from it. I feel neither here nor there, neither alive nor dead; it's a strange feeling but I think it's the only way my body and mind can now cope.

I don't use this word with ease or without thought and consideration to those who have genuinely experienced it, but it's the only word I can use to describe what this feels like and what it feels like…is torture.

Chapter Twenty-Seven

Beth.

The ten things you will feel as a caregiver:

- Regret – why didn't I push the doctors harder? Why didn't I do more research instead of work? Why didn't I take her to the private hospital sooner? Am I doing the right thing?
- Grief – for every bit of the person, future and time she's lost and as a result, what I've lost, too.
- Defensiveness – because everyone who's not looking after her is always full of advice for what I could be doing better.
- Worry – because all the worst ifs and buts have and could, very easily, come true.
- Powerless – because everything I do can never be enough.
- Resentment – at everyone and everything that's taken the life I'd planned away. For the huge responsibilities that have fallen at my feet and for the struggle I now have to cope with them.
- Anger – at the situation and that no one warned or highlighted this disease, that those doctors' ignorance has resulted in such profound suffering. Anger at

those who don't have to fight for their treatment, who are lavishly given care and support while the rest of us struggle for survival.

- Loneliness – because the person I once knew has been replaced by an unknowable stranger and because friends and even family don't understand the magnitude of what's going on.
- Guilt – for all the things I feel above.
- Pride – for the child who never gives up.

I spray some perfume on my neck before halting, frozen in my tracks…perfume gives Joyce headaches; I'll just have to wash it off when I get home, I tell myself. With a heavy sigh I dump the bottle back into my bag and rest my head against the headrest, drumming my restless fingers on the steering wheel. Perhaps I should go home, I think to myself, looking at the coffee shop across from me. It's only three in the afternoon. Joyce will think I'm still at work, so she won't know any different, I remind myself, but more than that, I'm terrified of disturbing her routine by coming home early…still, I can't shake the guilt I feel as I get out of the car and lock it before heading across the road to the coffee shop.

I'm spotted as soon as I enter and my two friends wave me over with broad smiles which ease my uncertainty. I smile as I make my way over, my shoulders relaxing as the tantalising smell of luxurious coffee and delicious cake takes me back to happier times.

'Hi,' I say airily, sitting in the empty chair between Liz and Cathy.

'We were beginning to think you were never coming,' Cathy says with a bright smile but a barbed tone.

'How are you?' Liz asks quickly.

The question catches me off guard. It shouldn't really, it's a common question but somehow it does.

'Yeah...fine, I'm fine,' I repeat as though to confirm it to both them and myself. 'What have you both been up to?'

'I was just telling Liz about my holiday to Croatia. Bill surprised me with a five-star hotel. It was just amazing...'

Cathy launches into her stories about her glorious holiday, pausing only when a waitress the same age as Joyce comes over to take our order. By the bored look on Liz's face I can tell she's already been treated to Cathy's holiday tales before I arrived. When the waitress serves us our coffee, Liz grabs the interruption in conversation to change the subject.

'Do you think that waiter over there is wearing any trousers?' she asks, pointing to the man in question.

I look over to see a man in his forties, wearing a tight white shirt, a red apron and...trainers.

'Ah wait, he's about to turn around,' Liz adds like a mischievous teenager.

We wait on tenterhooks for the moment to arrive...the waiter turns from the table he was tending to reveal that he's wearing a tiny pair of black shorts.

Liz bursts into laughter, her head tipping backwards in glee, before adding equally as loudly, 'I was worried about what we were going to see there.'

Liz and I are guffawing so loudly that Cathy looks around self-consciously as everyone turns to stare at us.

'Good on him,' Liz congratulates heartily, watching the man in the tiny shorts. 'Makes a change from young girls with their asses out.'

'I don't think that was an improvement,' Cathy says

disapprovingly. 'So what have you been up to, Beth?'

'Sorry, Cathy, what did you say?' I ask, reluctant to take the smile off my face.

'I said, what have you been up to?'

'Just work and looking after Joyce. She's only got a couple of weeks left on treatment,' I say.

'I bet she can't wait to get back to doing normal teenage things,' Cathy says, delicately sipping from her cup.

'I think it will be a while before she's doing that, but at least we're on the path there,' I say before asking the two of them, 'How's work going?'

We chat for ages. Catching up on each other's news or their news, I should say, seeing as I don't really have any.

'Shall we go for dinner after this?' Liz asks, finishing her cup.

'I can't, I need to get home to make Joyce's dinner,' I say disappointedly.

'Surely she can put a pizza in the oven,' Cathy remarks.

I stare at her in disbelief: how could this person have been so understanding, so patient and able to listen when I went through my divorce but when it comes to Joyce's illness, she's so damn flippant and dismissive?

'No, actually she can't,' I say sharply, all elation I felt before draining away.

'Well, we can go,' Cathy says to Liz, who looks less than pleased by the idea. 'You can decide where while I go to the ladies' room.'

'Are you ok?' Liz asks, as Cathy disappears to the bathroom.

'I'm fine,' I say meekly.

'Why don't we go away for the weekend to a spa or something? Just us, we can leave Gran at home,' Liz says, referring to Cathy.

'I can't leave Joyce at the moment,' I say heavy-heartedly.

'Ok, well, as soon as you can, just give me a call and I'll arrange everything.'

'Thanks. I'm going to head off before she comes back,' I say, getting up and hugging Liz goodbye.

'Ok, I'll tell her Mr Short Shorts whisked you away to Italy on a private jet for a five-star holiday,' Liz says in a wistful voice.

I laugh and wave goodbye as I head out of the door.

At home, I put Joyce's dinner plate by the sink; she's managed to eat most of it, but her weight's still dropping. I don't think she has much nausea on this treatment, which is one small mercy. I eat my dinner with a large glass of wine before washing the dishes and taking Dog out into the field beside the house. I miss my nightly runs but I don't like to leave Joyce along in the evenings – when she's so often at her worst.

With my mobile in one hand and the thrower in the other, I hurl Dog's ball across the field. He bounds after it, enthralled by the chase. Over and over again I throw his ball, until I'm mind-numbingly bored and he's tired. Then I take him and use the garden tap to hose him down: I don't like the idea that he could be carrying the very culprit of Joyce's misery into bed alongside her. I put stuff on Dog each month to kill any ticks that bite him, but even the best stuff takes 48 hours to kill the tick and in the meantime, you just have to hope you either find and remove it, or that it doesn't drop off onto your couch or carpet before the repellent has had time to kill it. Even with all my precautions, I still find ticks on him and each time it makes my heart go cold.

After drying Dog with a towel, I sit down at the kitchen table with a notepad, envelope and pen. I stare at the white paper with its faint blue lines until they dance before my eyes. I sigh heavily and pick up my pen, an anchor made of fear and anxious anticipation so deep inside of me it's created a cavern in my gut. I write to the only person who can understand:

'Dearest little sister' ... I pause, unsure of how to go on...

'You would be so proud if you could see your daughter now...'

I stop and stare at my own words: would my sister and brother-in-law feel proud or would they feel as scared as I do, a habitual and all-consuming terror? Would my sister's heart quicken each time she went near Joyce's room? Would her hands sweat as they reached out for the door handle as mine does? Would she pause each morning when she gives Joyce her supplies to gaze at her chest, waiting in the gloom...waiting in suspended time...for the movement that proves she's still breathing? Because I do, every day – that's how ill she's become and every day she gets worse, slipping into a world I fear I can't retrieve her from. I don't know if I'm saving her or killing her.

I scrunch up my letter and hurl it across the room. Dog diligently springs from his bed, his claws scraping and scrabbling across the tiles after it. He brings it to me and drops it gently onto my lap, his big, brown eyes looking up at me with such affection it's as though he understands and sympathises with all my woes. I pat him gently before carefully unscrunching the paper and neatly folding it into the envelope. I take it upstairs to my bedroom where I keep a box full of my letters to the dead. All of them are written to either my parents or my sister and her husband – who felt like a brother of my own. I add the latest letter to the rest and then run my finger over the tops of them, like little rungs on a ladder, but I don't feel the relief of unburdening that I usually feel, nor any comfort from my confession.

A little while later, I bring Joyce her allowed fruit for the day and then whittle away the time until she needs me next by watching TV and researching Herx reactions. It's terrified and haunted me ever since I read that in some cases the Herx reaction, which involves a build-up of toxins, can kill people. Over the past two and a half months I've phoned the private hospital numerous times, worried about how ill Joyce is, but they either don't realise how bad things are or are just so used to irate parents and family phoning in distress, because each time they give me the same advice…keep going for as long as she can take it; make sure she's drinking a lot; keep trying things to ease her discomfort.

But I don't know how to ease her pain. On top of everything else she feels, Joyce is often subjected to twitches. She's had them since she became ill, but their frequency and growing aggression frighten me; I know they frighten her, too – I can see it in her eyes. It's like she's a puppet, her limbs dancing to the pull of the string. It leaves her breathless, her limbs lifeless from exhaustion when it fades. I know the violence of the movements hurts her, for sometimes she can't help but cry as little moans escape her. And there's nothing I can do. I try to rub her limbs, unsure if I'm helping or hurting her more.

At suppertime, I make her cinnamon milk and then hold the cup for her as she drinks through a straw. After that I take her to the bathroom. It's the only time I ever really get to see her because her room is always in darkness – she doesn't even turn on the light beside her bed anymore. I help ease her onto the chair I put by the sink, my heart aching at the sight of someone once so beautiful and free...what is it doing to you? I question.

I'm not sure what's worst: the illness or the treatment or watching the battle as the two sides collide. Joyce is so hunched over that her chin only just comes up to the rim of the sink. All the colour and life has gone from her eyes; they seem glazed, unfocused as though she can't take in what's around her, and the area around them is so swollen with exhaustion that her eyes are mere slits. Her teeth have turned a vile shade of yellow. She has a painful-looking rash which turns to inflamed spots on her chest and back, as her body attempts any method to rid itself of the toxin within her: by pushing them out through her skin. She's so pale I can see the blue veins in her face. She's so thin and frail that I'm scared to touch her. Her once flowing auburn hair now hangs in unwashed clumps to her head. I brush it each night, being careful that the brush does not touch her sensitive scalp. When I'm done, I hide the brush before she can see how much of her hair has come away.

Once she's ready, I take her back to bed and tuck her in. I shut the door quietly and go to the sitting room whose curtains now always lie open, because Joyce doesn't ever come in here now. I look at the books on ME and Lyme, the stacks of paper I've printed for research, invoices and leaflets piled on the coffee table. On the TV they're showing a charity advert, guilt tripping people to donate to a disease known by all, a disease whose treatment is well funded by the public hospitals that should have treated Joyce. The public and government awareness campaign means that no one cannot know of its existence, it's an illness with so many charities to its name and so many support groups that it dominates all other diseases, whereas Lyme seems to be a state secret. In pure rage I swipe my arm along the coffee table, hurling all the books and papers across the room…but it's not enough to abate my fury: I want to scream and hurl everything in sight.

I stand there, breathing heavily as the advert comes to an end and quickly my belligerence turns to sorrow. I sit on the couch, my head in my hands as I cry. I know that disease is terrible, both my parents died from it, after all, but there are other illnesses out there which are equal if not worse. I hate myself for even thinking that if Joyce had the disease that the charity advertised, she would have been treated in a far better way. People would rally around her; they would shower her with sympathy and understanding; they would call her brave and courageous; they wouldn't question and judge her every move as a lie.

My mobile rings on the couch beside me and I swiftly answer it: from the silence at the other end of the line, I can tell that it's Joyce. I hasten through to her room as she finally manages to start speaking.

'I…heard…a, a bing…you ok?' she asks breathlessly, her voice so faint from weakness I have to strain to hear her.

I swallow the lump in my throat as I conclude she meant to say bang rather than bing. Every word is an effort for her, you can see it on her face as she tries to get her mind and mouth to work as one and the energy each letter takes just to say.

'Yes, I'm fine,' I say very slowly and carefully so that she can understand. 'I just dropped something. I'm sorry I disturbed you,' I say gently.

I go to her bed and carefully lie beside her. I go to put my arm around her, but I don't know what parts of her hurt, so I rest my hand on her waist – my hand disappearing between the sharp bones of her ribs and hip; I'm careful to keep the weight in my arm so that none of my weight is upon her. I gently kiss her bony shoulder – glad that, in the darkness and with her back to me, she can't see my tears fall because even with all the pain she's in, she still worries about mine.

Chapter Twenty-Eight

A little fuel for your fear:

- Everything about Lyme disease is contested – no sooner does a scientist prove or discover something about Lyme disease than ten more scientists appear to prove it wrong… only for it to frequently be proven right years later.

- What are my chances of getting Lyme? – I live in the city. Do you really think all those pigeons, foxes, rats and deer in your parks and cities don't get ticks? My aunt met a guy at the hospital who got Lyme by a tick bite on his rooftop garden…how? – you ask…birds! A massive study done by vets (not the government) recently proved that ticks are as prevalent in cities as they are in rural areas.

- If Lyme disease is so hard to get accurate blood results for and can lie dormant in the body for years…how can blood banks know without doubt that the blood they're infusing, into often immune compromised people, does not contain Lyme disease?

- If Lyme disease can infiltrate every part of the body: is it really safe to be eating rare and often still bloody beef and venison?

- If research is correct and Lyme has been found in human breast milk, then is it unrealistic to consider that it could be in cows' milk?

- If the above two points are correct, then is our stomach acid strong enough to kill the Lyme bacteria before it enters our bloodstream?
- Are female ticks that have Lyme transferring it to their young. Are we?
- If something is not done soon, is Lyme to be the next pandemic?

It started near the end of month four, when the medication had long since left my system. It began with feeding myself, going to the bathroom myself. Then the month ended with me washing myself with a face cloth and my aunt washing my hair for me over the bath.

At month five, I began making my own breakfast. Halfway through the month, I washed a glass each day…a week later I washed two. At the end of the month, I sat on a tall chair and managed to wash all the dishes. I walked down the two steps of the back door and the next day, I walked four. At the end of the month I walked to the bench, collapsing with the effort amidst the chill of the January breeze, until I'd recovered enough to walk back.

At month six, I showered myself, sitting at the bottom of the shower tray as the water ran luxuriously down my long hair and across my shoulders. Halfway through the month, I sit as my aunt tries her best to trim my scraggily hair. By the end of the month, I'm able to wander slowly around the back garden.

Each day I went against my body's desire to rest. Pushing myself each day to do things I felt incapable of doing, while at the same time trying to keep the balance of not doing too much and undoing what I'd achieved.

But a lot of the damage I never saw coming… it sprung upon me with an unexpected force I found I had no control over.

I pull back one side of my curtain, glad that the dullness of February allows me to do so. I'm about to head back to my sofa bed when I see a car I don't recognise pull into the drive. I hesitate, rigid with fear. I can't close the curtain now or they'll know there's someone inside. I duck down out of sight as I hear the car door shut. Then I crawl into the corner of my room, the crunch of gravel growing louder as the person approaches. I curl myself tightly into a ball, clamping my hands around my sensitive ears as the doorbell is rung. Go away, please go away, please go, I think over and over again as I press myself more tightly into the corner of my room – fear spiking into my chest as the doorbell is rung once more. After a fourth attempt at the doorbell, the person walks back to their car. Their shadow is projected onto the wall in front of me as they walk past my room; the dark shape moving towards me like a stealthy predator, creeping ever closer…until it disappears into the gloom of my room and is swallowed by the deep corners of darkness. The person drives off but I remain sitting on the floor, too scared to move. Until finally I'm certain the person's not coming back. Once I get myself off the floor, I slowly go to the window and peer outside – the grounds of my fortress free of invaders. I shut the curtain, shocked and afraid of what I've become.

A week later Aunt Beth comes home early from work. She puts her head around the door and smiles when she sees I'm awake.

'How are you feeling?' she asks.

'Fine,' I reply from my sofa bed.

'I thought maybe we could go for a short drive,' she suggests.

'I don't want to,' I say automatically, glancing at my closed curtains.

'Come on, we won't go far,' my aunt says with a conviction I know I won't overturn. She holds out her hand and, like an obedient toddler, I take it and allow her to lead me to the car.

I could refuse her; I keep forgetting I'm technically an adult but refusing would be too easy; it's going into the world which is hard.

'Are you not putting on your belt?' Aunt Beth asks as she shuts the driver's door and pulls her belt across her.

'Oh, yeah,' I say meekly, having forgotten something which was once automatic.

My aunt starts the car and heads out of the drive. I grab the outsides of my thighs as we head onto the main road: this isn't natural...I'm stationary but the world around me is moving. I watch the road advancing and disappearing under the bonnet of the car and ultimately under me. I lean away from the door of the car as a road sign, warning drivers about deer on the road, comes towards us. I squeeze my thighs tightly, flinching as the sign flies past us. I sigh quietly because I was sure it was going to hit us and smash through the windscreen. A lunatic driver overtakes us: I can't imagine what speed they must be going at to do so.

On the road ahead, a lorry hurls its way towards us on the other side of the road. Its huge, powerful front coming at us like a battering ram. I want to grab the wheel and pull us away from it, but my aunt is calm and utterly unfazed by the monstrosity. I lean away from it, my nails digging into my thighs as it thunders past us.

'It's all right,' my aunt tells me reassuringly. 'They built a new house up there, do you see it?' she asks, trying to distract me from the road.

'Yeah,' I say, glancing between the road and the world beyond it repeatedly.

It's jarring how the world's changed in the seven months since I left it completely. New houses and sheds have gone up; there are fences where there were none. The world when I left it was full of colour, the trees were green and leafy, plants had bloomed with flowers, the grass was green and youthful. Now the trees are skeletons stripped of flesh, the colourful flowers non-existent and the grass coarse and frostbitten. The animals within the fields move with the sluggish steps of winter, their spring and summer bounce long gone. I don't feel like I know this place anymore; I don't think I belong. Even the sun is a stranger to me now.

Another car overtakes us, then another. My nails dig into my thighs – the knowledge of unseen things happening behind us making me edgy.

'How fast are we going?' I ask.

'Ehh, about twenty miles per hour,' my aunt answers, glancing at the speedometer.

'What?' I splutter in disbelief. 'I-I was sure you were going at sixty.'

'It's just because you're not used to it,' my aunt says consolingly.

I think of the speed I've been travelling at over the past seven months and I wonder if I ever reached one mile per hour. By the time we get home, twenty minutes later, I feel as sore as I did after our five-hour drive to Northcairn.

Over the following few months I continue to play the game

of snakes and ladders. Each few days the roll of the dice moves me a place forward on the board which has no end, and each time I glimpsed the beam of progress, my next move sends me down the snake's neck. For every step of improvement I make, I'm knocked ten backwards. Only in this game of snakes and ladders there are only the snakes and the deep, dark holes at the end of each of their tails.

At least once a week my aunt makes a point of taking me out in the car, slowly extending the length of time that we drive. I hate every moment of it and I resent my body's punishment after it. Eventually my walking improves to the point where I can walk the same distance as I could before my treatment: in reality, it's not far but it's something. And every advance I make beyond that my aunt cheers on as though it's a great victory, but to me, it doesn't feel like something to celebrate because it's taken all I have, I've given it everything and all I feel upon achieving it is pain and exhaustion. There is no end in this game: each improvement simply means I must move on to the next. Perhaps I'll feel victory when I come to the end of a walk or activity and suddenly I realise…it was effortless.

Chapter Twenty-Nine

Five years later.

Stupid things healthy people say to sick people:

- Well, you look great; the picture of health – Ahh well, thanks, you know, you don't look like a moron but clearly looks can be deceptive.
- You're so lucky you get to watch TV all day – I'll let you into a little secret…daytime TV is only interesting and enjoyable if you're skiving off; otherwise, it's so mind-numbing it kills your brain cells.
- You don't look sick, you look great – although similar to the above, it does raise a different response: do tell, how exactly is a chronically sick person meant to look?
- You're so fortunate you don't have to go to work/uni – it's true, I am utterly blessed to be so unwell I can't function like a normal human being.
- I thought your house would be immaculate – firstly, that's just rude, and secondly, if I'm not well enough to work, why would you think I'm able to do house-WORK?
- You're so blessed to have this time being ill. You must have such unique experiences – if I hit you, can I claim it was mental incompetence? You're right, of course: I should be grateful for losing nearly a decade of my life

and for all the suffering I and my family have endured…
you dipstick.

- The only way to get better is to be positive – do you people never get bored of this mantra? It's bad enough when people I know say it to me, but you and I have literally just met! And by the way, who the heck are you to sit before me in your healthy frame and tell me to be positive?

- You should use this oil, it cures everything – Wow… it really cures everything! Is this the miracle cure coveted by all? And here I thought all the cancer, Huntington's, Parkinson's, dementia and all of the other diseases in the world had been cured by positivity.

- Oh, you were diagnosed privately, so which diagnosis do you think is correct? – hmm let me think… well it's tricky but could it be the private hospital which is independent and isn't influenced or financially bound by the government?

- Private, how are you paying for it? – Ehh, I'm pretty certain, it's none of your business!

- Hey, disabled parking's over there – firstly, child and parent parking spaces are NOT a legal requirement, they're a courtesy. You would think seeing as disabled parking *is* a legal requirement, that it would be given priority for the closest and safest parking spaces which don't require you to cross a busy road, but apparently not! Secondly, just who do you think is more likely to dodge an oncoming car? The healthy child or the sick/old person who can barely walk…hmm, it's tricky! Thirdly, I would like to point out that you choose to have children and then you choose to take them with you to the shops, whereas I don't have the luxury of leaving my little bundles of burdens at home or in the car!

• You can't be that ill if you can still have a laugh – parental scolding has left me disinclined to swear but…what the fuck? What do you people want? One minute I'm being told to be positive, to laugh my cares away and within the next minute, I'm being too positive to be as ill as I am. You can't win, so I say laugh in the moments you feel it, cry in the moments you need to, and don't ever let anyone make you feel bad for still having the ability to feel at all.

I sigh as I look at myself in the mirror in my bedroom. It feels odd to wear a dress after living in trousers for so long. The dress is fitted at the top and falls softly around my hips and legs, accentuating what little curves I have. From my neck down I could be someone healthy, but my face and the bags under my eyes are my undoing. My auburn hair is recently cut and freshly curled that day, my shortened hair makes the curls bounce and tickle my shoulders. I watch as I move my arms and legs as I straighten my dress and turn in the pretence of looking at the back of the dress in the mirror, but really I watch with fascination as my muscles move and stand out under my skin. I smile at them with pride, like a parent welcoming home a lost child, their absence greatly missed.

I take another deep breath, my stomach fluttering with anxiety. I look up as a burst of laughter filters into my room from outside, and for the first time in a long time I long to join the revelry. I head downstairs – patting Dog's head as he lies in his basket. Outside, the large gazebo consumes a large portion of the garden, music blares from within, and I check my musician's earplugs are fitted snugly in my ears before going inside. Fairy lights are strung all over the gazebo and banners announcing that it's Sarah's twenty-first birthday hang in numerous places.

I return to the table I was sitting at before one of Sarah's drunken friends spilt his drink down me and I had to change. The group of people sitting at the table has changed somewhat. I listen as they talk about a device for taking and sending pictures. They speak about things I've only vaguely heard of before, things that never existed before I was ill but are now commonplace.

'Hey, you want to dance?' one of the guys asks from further down the table. He's about the same age as me, with black hair and blue eyes.

'Sure,' I say brightly.

I'm about to get up when I see the drunk drink-spiller from earlier lean over the table to say something in his ear.

'She's Sarah's sick sister,' he says in a loud, drunken attempt at a whisper. 'Haha, she's four s's.'

The guy glances surreptitiously at me before looking back to his drunk friend and then saying to me, 'I think I'll sit this one out.'

I grab the nearly half-empty bottle of Cava off the table and head out of the gazebo. I jump up onto the garden wall, the twinkling fairy lights and lanterns strung about the garden standing out now the light's fading. I take a sip from the bottle, the bubbles fizzing in my mouth.

I've undergone three rounds of treatment in the last five years, each different to the other, but each came with crushing deterioration and each time I picked myself up, I pushed myself onwards, I rebuilt myself from scratch. I'm still taking countless supplements and I'm not sure if I'll end up on more antibiotic treatment soon but I suspect I will spend my life on and off them.

I can't say my life has changed all that much; things are still the same but they've altered somewhat. I now take Dog out for a walk every evening and every time I marvel at the glory of something so simple. I can now walk five miles without being bedbound afterwards. I'm doing one of the exams I missed out on in high school; I can't manage into college each day but I do the course by distance learning. What I will do at the end of the course, I don't know, because it's the only course you can do by distance learning, but maybe by then I'll be well enough to attend classes in college and if not, then perhaps my education will stagnate until I am well enough but I know I won't, because I'm doing things now I haven't done since before I was ill: I go out to lunch with Amy, just her and me, my bodyguards of Aunt Beth and Dog at home. I went canoeing with Logan and swimming with Sarah. I'm slowly building up to do all the things I once did and more.

I can't lie to you, it doesn't get any easier: the problems, the pain and the difficulties are all there, they're just different to what they were before. So, take the victories when you get them, I know they're bittersweet, I know winning often hurts as much as losing, but welcome them anyway – you've more than earned them.

I glance behind me as a loud burst of laughter sounds from within the gazebo and I catch a glimpse of Sarah dancing with her friends, my cousin Kate and her fiancé dancing alongside her. I've wondered many times since they announced their engagement what my future relationships might be like. If there will ever be anyone willing to share their lives with me and the monster within. How would I ever explain what I've been through when I don't understand myself? My life will forever be tainted by this disease. I am adult now and yet I'm warped, so often I feel sixteen and I have to remind myself that I'm not a child anymore – I'm not even a teenager. It's like I've woken up one day having time-travelled nearly ten years into the future: technology, social media, the way people speak, dress, behave; application forms and books on screens; it's all changed without me, but I am learning to catch up.

'You throwing yourself a party?' someone familiar says, with a laugh I know that I know.

'Perhaps,' I say with a bright smile, watching as the figure comes out of the shadows and into my view, lit by the fairy lights dancing around me.

I jump down from the wall and throw my arms around Logan.

'You came,' I say exuberantly.

'I said I would,' he says cheerfully.

'You said you'd try and come. You want some?' I say, holding out the bottle.

He takes it from me and we sit on the wall, sharing the rest of the bottle between us.

'So why are you hiding out here?' he asks.

'I'm not hiding. I'm just not drunk enough to not care about the people in there,' I say, taking a gulp and handing him the bottle.

'Why, what happened?' Logan asks, the fairy lights shining off his brown eyes.

'No one wants to dance with the sick girl,' I explain, pleasantly tipsy; years of being teetotal has left me a lightweight.

'Oh shut up. No one thinks that,' Logan retorts good-naturedly.

'I have been ditched twice tonight by guys who found out I

was ill. One of them was chatting me up for at least an hour, until Sarah came up to us and said how proud she was of me to be well enough to organise her party and how ill I'd been…and I've not see him since,' I say, swaying a little on the wall. 'And the other asked me to dance until Sarah's drunk friend told him I was sick and suddenly he changed his mind.'

'Oh yeah, ok, you've been ditched,' Logan concedes, handing me back the last of the bottle. 'Go on, you've won the right to drink the rest.'

'You know, drinking legally kind of takes the fun out of drinking,' I say, making Logan roar with mirth.

'It does a bit. Listen, I know it's a rubbish consolation but you look…nice,' he says.

'Nice…wow, thanks. Nice was really what I was aiming for,' I say teasingly.

'You know what I mean. You look…you look beautiful,' Logan says awkwardly.

'Thank you,' I say gratefully.

'Come here,' Logan says, jumping down from the wall and holding out his hand for me to take.

'Why?' I ask suspiciously.

'Because, we're going to dance…if you're up for it?' he adds quickly.

I smile and jump off the wall. Taking his hand, we head into the gazebo and Logan twirls me as we go onto the grassy dance floor. Sarah spots us and heads over, the three of us dancing together. The song quickly finishes and the next one soon follows.

'I'm going to get Aunt Beth,' Sarah calls excitedly.

Sarah disappears into the crowd as everyone in the tent, young and old, recognises the song. The gazebo erupts into noise and movement as everyone jumps up and down in time to the music, and as everyone yells the words excitedly at each other. Sarah appears with Aunt Beth, Kate and her partner who seems rather baffled by the sudden eruption but is joining in nonetheless. The six of us leap up and down, shouting the words as loud as we can. My legs start humming from the effort but I don't stop, because for now, I know that I'm stronger than my weakness and for the first time in nearly ten years, I'm dancing. With Sarah, Aunt Beth, Kate and Logan by my side and right now, in this very moment, nothing can subdue…my Joy.